EXCITEMENT, SUSPENSE—AND KAY TRACEY—GO TOGETHER!

Sixteen-year-old Kay Tracey is an amateur detective with a sense of sleuthing that a professional might envy. Her closest friends who share her adventures are Betty Worth and her twin sister Wendy. Whenever there is a mystery in the small town of Brantwood, you'll find Kay and her two friends in the middle of it.

If you like spine-tingling action and heart-stopping suspense, follow the trail of Kay and her friends in the other books in this series: *The Double Disguise, In the Sunken Garden, The Six Fingered Glove Mystery, The Mansion of Secrets,* and *The Green Cameo Mystery.*

A Kay Tracey Mystery

THE MESSAGE
IN THE
SAND DUNES

Frances K. Judd

A BANTAM SKYLARK BOOK

THE MESSAGE IN THE SAND DUNES
A Bantam Skylark Book/published by arrangement with Lamplight Publishing, Inc.

PRINTING HISTORY
Hardcover edition published in 1978 exclusively by Lamplight Publishing, Inc.
Bantam Skylark edition/October 1980

ISBN 0-553-15072-3

Published simultaneously in the United States and Canada

Bantam Books are published by Bantam Books, Inc. Its trademark, consisting of the words "Bantam Books" and the portrayal of a bantam, is Registered in U.S. Patent and Trademark Office and in other countries. Marca Registrada. Bantam Books, Inc., 666 Fifth Avenue, New York, New York 10103.

PRINTED IN THE UNITED STATES OF AMERICA

0 9 8 7 6 5 4 3 2 1

BOOK DESIGNED BY MIERRE

Contents

THE MESSAGE
IN THE
SAND DUNES

"I'll tell you!" the woman cried, not
recognizing Kay.

I

Gathering Driftwood

"Listen to the roar of those waves!" Kay Tracey shouted, hurrying from her seaside cottage with Betty and Wendy Worth.

"I think we're going to have a hurricane," blond Betty remarked, turning her face away from the howling wind.

Her twin sister Wendy agreed, adding, "We'd better gather that driftwood in a hurry. We'll need two loads to keep our fire going tonight."

Trudging through the sand, the three stooped to gather sticks and old weathered pieces of timber.

"I don't like the seashore in a storm," Wendy said, looking up at the low-scudding clouds, "especially at Seaside Beach, with all those strange characters roaming around."

"You mean the beachcombers?" Kay asked.

"Yes, and those two strange old women."

"The Crowley sisters are harmless," Kay replied.

"All they need is broomsticks and they'd zoom over the beach," Betty said, pretending to shiver.

Their arms loaded with wood, they started back to the cottage, which had been rented by Kay's mother. Mrs. Tracey had gone to a nearby town for groceries, and Kay's cousin, Bill, a young lawyer who lived with them, had driven back to their hometown of Brantwood on business.

By the time the girls reached the door of their cottage, the surf was thundering on the white sand, sending salt spray high into the air. The beach itself was deserted.

"I hope your mother comes home soon," Wendy said, depositing her armful of wood in a box beside the fireplace.

"She'll be back by the time we gather our second load of driftwood," said Kay confidently, tossing another log onto the crackling blaze.

By now the wind had reached a steady whine and was rattling the windows.

"I wish you hadn't mentioned witches," Wendy told her sister. "I keep thinking of those Crowley sisters. How can they live in a lonely place like this all winter long?"

"They just tighten their shutters and sit it out, I guess," Kay laughed.

"And pet their black cats," Betty teased.

By this time all the wood had been stacked neatly in the box and they prepared to set out again, when suddenly they were startled by a knock on the door.

Recovering from her surprise, Kay Tracey went to the door and opened it. A boy of perhaps sixteen, dressed in grimy trousers which were wet to the knees, stood on the porch. His sandy hair was rumpled, his eyes were bloodshot, and he seemed almost too tired to speak.

"What is it?" Kay questioned kindly.

"Please, could you spare something to eat?" the boy asked.

Kay hesitated because she had been warned by her mother to be careful about taking beachcombers into the house. The boy seemed to sense her feeling.

"This is the first time I've ever begged for food,"

he said earnestly. "I wouldn't do it now, only I'm half starved. I have no money to pay you, but I'll give you something else which is worth more than what the food costs."

He groped in his pocket for something. Kay waved aside the gesture.

"You don't have to pay me," she said gently.

The boy followed her into the warm cottage, fumbling awkwardly as he became aware of Wendy and Betty, who stared at him curiously.

"Just sit here by the fireplace," Kay suggested, pulling up a chair. "I'll fix you a cup of coffee and some food."

While she busied herself at the stove, Wendy and Betty tried to draw him into conversation. He told them his name was Ben Wheeler and that he came from the west.

"Have you been beachcombing?" Betty asked.

The boy nodded. "I've picked up a few things along the shore, but the old-timers seem to get in ahead of me. Today I spent over twelve hours hunting in the sand and didn't find anything."

"It must be discouraging," Betty commented.

By this time Kay had prepared a warm lunch. She placed it before the boy who, after washing his face and hands at the kitchen sink, devoted himself to the meal. Twice Kay filled his plate. Finally he seemed to have satisfied his hunger.

"That was the best meal I ever tasted," he told Kay gratefully.

He got up as if to leave; then, to the astonishment of the girls, he took a bracelet set with glittering rhinestones from his pocket and dropped it carelessly on the table.

"This is to pay for the food," he said.

Kay stared at the jewelry. "Oh, I can't take that."

"It didn't cost me anything," he replied gruffly. "I picked it up on the beach along with a few other things."

Kay examined the bracelet with interest, then handed it back to him. With a shrug he thrust it into his pocket again.

"Suit yourself, but I'd like to have you keep it."

Wendy, who had been standing by the window, now interrupted the conversation.

"If we don't hurry and gather that driftwood it'll be too late. It's going to rain any minute."

"Yes, we'd better get going," Kay agreed, looking suggestively at Ben Wheeler, who continued to loiter.

"Say, if you need wood let me help gather it," he offered eagerly. "I'd like to do something to pay for the food. I can haul in logs for you."

"That's very nice of you," Kay replied. "We really do need a lot of fuel. These storms often last for days."

The girls closed the cottage door behind them and, with Ben Wheeler, set out across the beach. Soon the baskets were filled with wood, and Ben found several large logs which had been washed up by the waves and were now quite dry.

"I'll drag these big chunks to the cottage and come back for the baskets," he told Kay.

Waiting for Ben to return, the girls piled driftwood in one heap where it could be transferred quickly to the baskets. Then Kay noticed in the distance two elderly women in black with shawls tied over their shoulders, searching the beach for fuel. Kay had seen them several times before and knew that they were two sisters, Henrietta and Maud Crowley, who lived in a cottage nearby. The shabbily dressed ladies appeared to be nearly seventy years old, and the girls felt that the women should not be out in the stiff wind, much less attempting to lift heavy pieces of driftwood. Kay went over to them.

"Won't you take some of our wood?" she asked politely, pointing to the large pile. "We have much more than we need."

"Thank you, no," said Maud Crowley firmly.

"You are very kind," her sister added in a gentle voice, "but we have always gathered our own wood. We need no help."

Picking up their baskets, the two sisters moved farther down the beach. Kay returned to her friends.

"I guess I only drove them away. They're very proud and sensitive."

"Let's scatter some of our best wood where they'll find it when they return to their cabin," Wendy suggested. "I'm sure it'll start raining in another ten minutes. They can't fill their baskets in that time."

The girls tossed several of the chunks into the sand and then continued to impatiently wait for Ben Wheeler.

"He's had enough time to make three trips," Kay remarked, irritated. "What's keeping him?"

"Maybe he decided he didn't want to help us after all," Betty declared, looking anxiously at the darkening sky. "If we don't want to get drenched, we'll have to carry this fuel ourselves."

Wendy and Betty took the baskets, while Kay filled her arms with the extra pieces of driftwood. The wood was heavy and they walked slowly. Before they reached the cottage the first large drops of rain had begun to fall.

"Just in time," Wendy commented. "If we had waited for that boy the storm would have caught us."

"The Crowley sisters will be soaked for sure," Kay said, glancing back over her shoulder. "They're still far down the beach."

Nearing the cottage, the girls saw that Ben Wheeler had hauled the heavy logs onto the porch. The boy was nowhere to be seen.

"I guess he decided to move on and let us finish it on our own," Wendy said, setting down her basket.

"He could have told us he didn't intend to come back!"

Kay dumped her wood on the porch and opened the kitchen door, which had been left unlocked. Betty and Wendy heard her gasp.

"Oh no!" Kay cried. "The house has been robbed!"

The Worth twins ran to their friend's side. As the door swung back they saw that everything was in confusion. Chairs had been overturned, contents of drawers and cupboards had been spilled on the floor, and even clothing had been jerked from hangers.

"Someone has robbed the house!" Kay gasped again. "I should never have left the place unlocked."

"We were gone only a few minutes," Betty murmured. "I bet every cent of our money has been stolen!"

They ran from room to room. Even a casual glance showed that the entire house had been ransacked. Kay ran to the kitchen cupboard. She remembered that her mother had left ten dollars for groceries in a convenient sugar bowl. The container was still in the cupboard, but it was empty.

"My bag is missing!" Wendy exclaimed before Kay could say anything. "I left it in the drawer of this cabinet. It's not here now."

"Now I understand why that boy didn't return for the baskets of wood," exclaimed Betty. "He was too busy gathering up our money!"

"He may not be the thief—" Kay began, but the twins paid no heed to her.

"This is the way he repays us," Betty said bitterly. "And we listened to his story!"

A brief search convinced Kay that other hidden money had been taken from the house. On arriving at the cottage Mrs. Tracey had put money in several places. Fortunately the largest amount was still safe, but various small sums amounting to thirty dollars had been taken. Kay moved toward the door, her face stern and determined.

"Where are you going?" Wendy asked quickly.

"If Ben Wheeler is responsible for this, he can't be far away," Kay replied. "I'm going to bring him back!"

II

Battling the Storm

Wendy and Betty tried to get Kay to stay by warning her that the storm might break at any moment.

"It doesn't matter if I get drenched," Kay insisted as she hurried out on the porch. "I have to find that boy and question him."

"Here, wear my slicker," Betty urged, thrusting the garment into her hands.

Kay slipped into the raincoat and then ran down the beach. The wind tore at her golden hair, whipping it wildly about her face. Huge drops of rain fell, making deep pits in the furrows of sand.

Far ahead of her Kay saw a dark form approaching. For an instant she thought it might be Ben Wheeler. Then she saw two people whom she recognized as the Crowley sisters, hurrying toward their little home in the pine grove. Their heads were bent low and they seemed to be having difficulty in carrying their heavy baskets of wood. They did not see Kay until she was near enough to greet them by name.

"Have you seen Ben Wheeler anywhere on the beach?" Kay asked, shouting to make herself heard above the roar of wind and waves.

"Ben Wheeler?" Maud Crowley quavered as she put down her load.

"A boy of sixteen," Kay explained quickly. "He was dressed in shabby clothing, and——"

She broke off in confusion, realizing that she'd been thoughtless. The Crowley sisters also wore clothes that could be described as shabby. They did not appear to take offense, however. Actually, they had paid little attention to Kay's words because their attention was centered on the weather.

"We have seen no one," Maud replied hastily. She stooped to raise the basket of wood. "Pardon us for not stopping to talk, but the rain——"

Even as she spoke a gust of wind struck the three, fairly pushing them forward. Kay had difficulty maintaining her balance and the frail old ladies clung together for support.

"I'll help you with your wood," Kay offered, because she saw that the women could not handle the baskets alone.

This time the Crowley sisters were too tired to protest. Kay walked ahead of the old ladies, trying to shield them from the wind.

The sky had grown black as night, but for a moment longer the storm held off. Only a few drops of rain spattered down, and Kay hoped that they might reach the house before the torrent descended. A vivid flash of lightning streaked across the dark sky, followed by a deafening clap of thunder.

Henrietta clutched her sister's arm, crying out in terror. "Oh, that was close!" she shrieked.

"It struck a tree up on the hill," Kay said uneasily.

She did not urge the sisters to hurry. She knew that they were walking as fast as they possibly could.

The little house in the cluster of pine trees now was close by. Yet before the three could reach it, the rain came down in torrents. Then a flash of lightning severed the inky sky. It was so brilliant that it illuminated the path for a great distance. Kay saw fire everywhere. She staggered as if from an impact—and blacked out.

Unaware that their friend and the two old ladies had been stunned by a bolt of lightning, Wendy and Betty anxiously waited at the cottage.

"Kay will never find Ben Wheeler now," Wendy observed as she stood at the window. "This storm is terrible. I wish she would come back."

"She'll be drenched," Betty agreed. "But you know how Kay is—she'll never quit searching until she finds the thief who stole our money."

The Worth twins had grown up with Kay in Brantwood and were her most loyal friends. In appearance as well as disposition, Wendy and her sister were opposites. Betty was a blond while Wendy was a brunette. Betty loved a good time and was not as studious as Wendy, who took life very seriously and spent her free time writing poetry.

It did not occur to either of them that Kay might have met with an accident. In every emergency up till now she had been self-sufficient and resourceful.

Recently Kay had awed her friends with the skill she had shown solving mysteries which had baffled professional detectives. The young detective was not only glad to come up with the answers to intricate situations, but also happy to help people whose well-being depended upon the solution.

As Betty and Wendy Worth watched the storm from the cottage window, Kay and the Crowley sisters lay unconscious on the beach. A tall pine tree nearby had been felled by a bolt of lightning, whose electrical charge had stunned the three.

The rain fell in torrents. Kay, stirring slightly, could feel water trickling over her face. For several moments she could not remember where she was or what had happened. Little by little, however, her memory returned and she became aware of the Crowley sisters lying unconscious beside her.

Kay struggled to her feet and looked frantically about for help. No one was nearby. In her unsteady condition she knew she could not carry the two women to the house in the pines.

She dropped down on her knees beside Henrietta. The old lady stirred and mumbled to herself. To her relief Kay realized that the rain was helping to revive the woman. Maud seemed to be in a more serious condition. She did not move.

Ignoring the downpour, Kay began to apply artificial respiration. Soon she was elated to see that the woman seemed to be breathing regularly again. By this time Henrietta had struggled to a sitting position. She gazed about in bewilderment.

"What happened?" she murmured. "Were we struck by an automobile?"

"Not by an automobile," Kay corrected as she worked over Maud. "It was lightning, and we're lucky to be alive."

"Oh, I seem to remember now—we were hurrying to get out of the storm." Henrietta's gaze fell upon the prostrate figure of her sister and she gave a gasp of horror. "Maud! She's been killed!"

"Only stunned, as we were. I think she's regaining consciousness now, but we must get her to the house. I wish someone would come!"

Kay knew that Maud could not be of any help since the poor woman could scarcely stand up. She didn't want to leave the two sisters alone while she ran for help. As she debated what to do, a figure loomed up through the rain and a boy's voice called out:

"Hello there, what's wrong?"

"We need help!" Kay cried.

The boy hurried up, but not until he was close beside her did Kay realize he was Ben Wheeler. For an instant she forgot the Crowley sisters and their urgent need of attention. She sat back on her heels and stared blankly at the stranger.

"After robbing our cottage you had the nerve to return!" she shouted accusingly.

"I don't know what you're talking about," he replied tersely.

He helped Kay raise Maud to a sitting position and slipped his ragged coat over the old woman's shoulders to protect her from the rain.

"We have to get them to the house in the pine grove," Kay said anxiously. "Will you help me?"

"Of course I will. What do you think I am, anyway?"

Kay remained silent.

"You mentioned a robbery," he went on in an insistent tone. "Do you think I stole something from your cottage?"

"Someone did. You went there alone with wood and didn't come back."

"That was because I remembered I had another errand. I left the logs on the porch."

"You did not go in the cottage?"

"Of course I didn't. If the place has been robbed, I don't know anything about it."

Kay was mystified by Ben Wheeler's denial. If he was actually the thief, she did not think he would admit his guilt; yet it seemed amazing that he would return to face an accuser. He might be telling the truth.

"We won't talk about it right now," she told him quietly. "Just help me get this lady to the house."

Henrietta Crowley was able to walk unassisted. She followed Kay and Ben Wheeler, who supported her sister between them.

The rain had slackened a little, and through the trees Kay glimpsed the Crowley home. Smoke was coming from beneath the roof!

"The house has been struck by lightning!" she cried in horror. "It's on fire!"

III

The Secret Cupboard

Confronted with this latest disaster, Maud Crowley began to weep while her sister pleaded with Kay and Ben Wheeler to save their home.

"Everything we have in the world is in that house," cried Maud.

Leaving Henrietta to care for her sister, Kay and Ben darted into the burning building. A glance assured Kay that only the roof was on fire, and she hoped that the falling rain would keep the flames under control. With no ladders available, it was practically impossible for them to reach the roof until fire fighters arrived.

They seized various pieces of furniture and carried them outside. The furniture was old but the pair could tell it was far from worthless. The Crowley sisters had preserved family heirlooms which were now valuable antiques.

A large oak cupboard caught Kay's attention. It was too heavy to move, but she thought that if valuables were inside she might be able to save them. The doors were not locked, but they were slightly warped and resisted her efforts as she tugged at the knobs.

"Don't open that cupboard!" commanded a voice directly behind her. "Leave it alone!" Startled, Kay spun around and saw Henrietta Crowley.

"Save the clock," Henrietta ordered in an excited voice. "I'll attend to the cupboard myself."

"You shouldn't try to help," Kay protested. "You're not able——"

"I know my own strength," Henrietta interrupted firmly. "I'll look after the cabinet."

Kay moved away quickly, wondering why the woman didn't want her to open the doors. She saw Ben Wheeler peering curiously at the massive piece of furniture. He had heard Miss Crowley's words, and his own curiosity had been aroused.

Although Henrietta had declared that she would take care of the contents of the cupboard, she made no attempt to open it in the presence of Kay and Ben. Did she intend to wait until no one could watch her? Kay could not understand the woman's strange attitude.

The house was filling with smoke, but the fire had been waging a losing battle with the rain. As Kay carried a chair outside she glanced toward the roof and saw that the flames were still confined to a small area.

"The house may be saved after all!" she thought optimistically. "If only we had a ladder!"

Before Kay could reenter the house, she heard a shout from the road. An automobile drove up. From it jumped Mrs. Tracey and the Worth twins who came running toward her.

"We saw the fire from our cottage window!" Betty cried. "Your mother arrived just in time to bring us here."

"Oh, Mother, there's a chance to save the house if only help will come!" Kay exclaimed excitedly. "We need ladders and men to fight the fire!"

"I'll drive to the village, Kay."

Mrs. Tracey did not waste words but hurried back to the car. Wendy and Betty began to help Kay and Ben remove furniture from the house. The Crowley sisters were constantly in the way, but when Betty tried to get them to remain outside, they stubbornly refused.

Kay meant to warn her friends to avoid going near the oak cupboard but before she could say anything to them, Wendy had tried to open the doors.

"No! No!" Maud cried in a shrill voice. "Do not touch the cupboard!"

"I only wanted to help," Wendy said, backing away. .

In a short time Mrs. Tracey returned to the scene with the fire fighters. Men scrambled up on the roof to beat out the flames. Soon it was obvious that there was no need to carry out any more furniture because the house would be saved.

Exhausted, Kay and the twins took a brief rest. Mrs. Tracey persuaded the Crowley sisters to sit in her car where they would be protected from the rain.

As Kay watched the fire fighters extinguishing the last of the flames, she became aware that Ben Wheeler was nowhere to be seen. She wondered if he had slipped away to avoid questioning regarding the robbery. Stepping to the door of the house, she peered inside.

"Ben Wheeler!" she exclaimed. "What are you doing?"

He sprang away from the oak cupboard, but Kay knew that he had been attempting to open the doors.

"Why, I—I wasn't doing anything," he stammered in embarrassment.

Before Kay could say another word he had slipped out the door. She was tempted to follow him, but was too exhausted to make the effort.

"I'll probably be sorry I let him escape," she thought wearily. "I bet he's a thief."

In a few minutes the fire had been extinguished completely and the Crowley sisters' furniture was moved back into the house. Kay and the twins took dry cloths and wiped the water from the fine pieces.

"Luckily these antiques haven't been ruined," Kay observed in relief, "but the house is a mess. The rugs are caked with mud and the upstairs will have to be reroofed before it can be used."

"Henrietta and Maud never will be able to spend the night here," Wendy agreed, glancing about the wrecked interior. "Where will they go?"

Mrs. Tracey solved the problem by inviting the sisters to come to her cottage and remain there until their own place could be thoroughly cleaned and repaired. The Crowley sisters thanked her but said very firmly that they could accept no further aid.

"But where will you sleep?" Mrs. Tracey protested, amazed at their refusal.

"We can manage," Maud said quietly.

"Yes, we will set up our beds on the first floor," Henrietta added. "Please don't worry about us. We have always looked after ourselves."

"We are most grateful to you and your daughter for all you have done," Maud Crowley assured Mrs. Tracey hastily, fearing that she might misunderstand her attitude, "but there is nothing more either of you can do."

Kay's mother was very distressed and might have pressed the issue had Kay not given her a warning glance. In the end they decided to give in to the proud sisters. Before leaving the Crowleys alone, however, they decided to do everything possible to make the house livable again. While Mrs. Tracey and the girls were cleaning the lower floor, Kay was astonished to see Ben Wheeler coming up the path toward the house.

"Why, I thought he ran away," she told herself. "Maybe I misjudged him."

The young man appeared at the doorway to offer his services. Mrs. Tracey, who did not know of his attempt to open the cupboard, immediately accepted his aid. He was very good at lifting heavy pieces of furniture, though Kay watched him carefully to make certain that he took nothing from the house.

While the group was hard at work, an automobile drove up the road and stopped not far from the Crowley home. A smartly dressed man of fifty, his neatly pressed suit shielded from the rain by a huge umbrella, got out and came up the path. Not until he stood in the open doorway was he noticed by those in the house.

"Hello," he said in a cheerful voice, "it looks as if you've had a fire here."

Before Kay or her mother could reply, Henrietta Crowley, who had been shivering in a chair by the kitchen stove, got up with a startled cry.

"Peter Wake!" she exclaimed, her hands twisting nervously.

The man looked quickly about the room, and as he did so it seemed to Kay that his eyes gleamed with satisfaction as he scanned the wrecked interior.

"I see I'm needed here—" he began, but Maud interrupted in a shrill tone:

"No! No! We don't need help!"

"All of you must leave," Henrietta added, growing distressed. "Please—there is nothing more you can do."

Mrs. Tracey didn't want to leave the two old ladies alone, but in the face of such a firm request she could not force herself upon them. Their strange, aloof attitude completely baffled her.

Peter Wake did not follow the girls as they left the house with Kay's mother and Ben Wheeler. It was obvious that he wanted to speak with the Crowley sisters alone. From their nervous manner it was obvious that they were distressed by the man's presence.

As the others walked down the path toward Mrs. Tracey's car, Kay loitered near the door. She heard Peter Wake say to the Crowleys:

"This place is completely ruined. You have no choice now but to leave."

"No! No!" Maud cried in quick protest. "Please don't bother us! Let us remain here in peace!"

Kay didn't hear any more, because her companions were waiting for her. As Wendy and Betty walked on with Ben Wheeler, she caught up with her mother and they talked in low voices. Mrs. Tracey had learned all the details of the robbery from the twins and knew that the young man with them was under suspicion.

"I don't believe Ben Wheeler had anything to do with it," she told Kay decisively. "If he were guilty he would never have remained to face you."

"He may be a good actor."

"That's true, but I can't believe he entered the house. He doesn't act like a thief."

"No one else seemed to be in the vicinity at the time. Ben denies that he had anything to do with the robbery but I noticed he kept looking at that cupboard."

"I saw you gazing at it rather intently yourself," Mrs. Tracey said, smiling broadly.

"I admit the charge," Kay laughed, "but at least I didn't try to open the doors after I was warned away."

"You saw Ben do that?"

"I am certain he would have looked inside the cupboard if I hadn't been there."

"I may be mistaken about the young man," Mrs. Tracey said slowly. "After all, we know nothing about him. As you say, he may be a clever actor."

"I think we should question him and try to make him prove his story."

Mrs. Tracey nodded. "We'll ask him to come with us to our cottage, Kay."

"And if he refuses?"

"Then we must call the police."

IV

A Suspicious Character

Somewhat to the surprise of Kay and her mother, Ben Wheeler offered no objection when they suggested that he return with them to their cottage. He claimed to be amazed at the robbery.

"I hope you don't think I had anything to do with it," he said. "I wouldn't do a mean trick like that—not after I'd been given a good meal."

"Did you notice that the door was unlocked?" Kay questioned.

"Sure, I knew you didn't lock it, but I didn't go inside. I just left the wood on the porch."

"Did you see anyone around when you were there?"

Ben shook his head.

Kay realized that she was getting nowhere with the questioning. If Ben Wheeler had taken the money from the cottage he was far too shrewd to admit anything damaging to himself. She thought that the police might do better, and using the excuse that she needed Ben's help to report the story to local authorities, persuaded him to come with them to the police station. There Kay offered her scant evidence and Ben was subjected to severe questioning from Chief Benson. He was ready with frank answers to all their interrogations.

By this time even kindhearted Mrs. Tracey had grown suspicious of him. Yet, without any real evidence, it was impossible to accuse him of being a housebreaker.

"Just what was taken from the cottage?" asked one of the police captains as he prepared to write down a detailed report of the case.

Wendy and Betty had made a careful check during Kay's absence and were ready with their list. In addition to the thirty dollars, a bracelet belonging to Kay, a pearl brooch, and an inexpensive watch owned by Bill Tracey had also disappeared.

"Will you pay money to get your things back?" Ben asked, turning to Mrs. Tracey. "How much reward are you offering?"

"I hadn't thought about that," she answered, studying him curiously.

"So you're interested in a reward, eh?" the policeman inquired dryly. "Maybe you know where to find some of the loot."

"Not offhand," Ben retorted brazenly. "But if a reward is offered I might be able to find all your things."

"The jewelry isn't of great value," Mrs. Tracey said after a moment of reflection. "I wouldn't be willing to pay more than twenty-five dollars to get it back."

Ben Wheeler looked disappointed.

"Well, I'll hunt for the stuff," he declared with a slight shrug.

"Where do you plan to search?" Kay inquired dryly.

"Oh, maybe in the woods. The thief may have hidden his loot close by the cottage."

"I can't imagine a robber being so stupid," Kay replied coldly. "But I hope you find it."

Ben followed Mrs. Tracey and the girls from the police station, parting with them when they went to their car.

"I'll get busy right away," he promised Kay. "I'm going straight to the woods now. The rain has let up and I'll be able to search for an hour or so before dark."

He raised his hat and slouched off down the street.

"A very obliging young man," Betty remarked sarcastically.

"Almost too obliging," Kay agreed. "If he comes walking in with that jewelry tomorrow I'll be sure he was the one who stole it."

"I'll bet he hid it in the woods himself," Wendy declared indignantly. "I don't see why the police didn't arrest him."

"Under the circumstances that was impossible," said Mrs. Tracey. "However, I noticed that the police chief watched Ben very closely. I wouldn't be surprised if he keeps an eye on him for the next few days."

Mrs. Tracey and the girls drove back to their cottage, dismissing Ben Wheeler from their thoughts for the time being. In the meantime he had set off in the direction of the woods. When he was certain that he was not being followed, he turned and walked toward the Crowley house. Approaching the place quietly, he tiptoed up to the rear window, and with his face flattened against the pane, peered inside.

"I'd like to know what's hidden in that cupboard," he muttered. "Maybe one of the old ladies will open it up."

Ben watched for several minutes as the two women moved about in the living room. Suddenly he felt himself grasped by the collar. Whirling about in terror, the boy found himself face to face with a burly, rough-looking man in cap and rain-soaked overcoat.

"Hi, pal!" greeted the man, giving Ben a hearty slap on the back. "See anything worth grabbing?"

"Oh, it's you, Smoky Rover," Ben said, his relief tinged with wariness.

"What's so interesting inside?" the heavyset man demanded, peering through the window.

"Why, n-nothing. I was just looking."

Smoky Rover grabbed Ben roughly by the shoulder. "You and me are pals—understand? If you try to hold out on me——"

"Honest, Smoky, I was just walking along here and all at once I thought I'd look in the window. I'm telling you the truth, Smoky. Come on, now, let's go back to camp."

The pair retreated a short distance from the cottage, but when they were sheltered by the trees the older man whirled savagely upon Ben Wheeler and began to choke him.

"You dirty little liar!" he said viciously. "I know you're up to something, and I'll get it out of you if I have to squeeze it out!"

"Quit—you're choking me," Ben cried, struggling to free himself. "Let me go! I'll tell everything!"

Smoky Rover released his hold.

"Two old ladies live in the cottage," Ben explained. "They have something hidden in a cupboard."

"How do you know?"

"This afternoon the house caught fire and I helped carry out the furniture. The women wouldn't let me touch the cupboard and guarded it to make sure no one looked inside."

"I knew you were up to something," Smoky Rover declared. "Thought you'd get it all for yourself, didn't you?"

"I was just curious, Smoky. I didn't intend to break into the house."

"Well, we'll just look into that cupboard and find out what the old women are hiding. It may be worth our time, eh?"

Smoky Rover turned as if to retrace his steps to the cottage. Ben held back, obviously frightened.

"It's dangerous," he protested.

"What do you mean?"

"There's a man—I don't know his name—but he seems to be their guardian. Anyway, he was at the cottage this afternoon."

"Why didn't you tell me that in the first place?" Smoky Rover demanded irritably. "You'd stand by and let a guy walk straight into trouble."

"I've been trying to tell you, Smoky."

"We'll let the cupboard go until I've had a chance to study this more," the older man said after a moment of thought. "Come on, let's get back to camp for some grub."

The pair made their way to a site nearby where they had parked a dilapidated car and a battered house trailer. Smoky Rover stretched himself comfortably on the bed as he ordered his young companion to prepare supper.

Back at the Tracey cottage, Kay and her mother were fixing their own evening meal when a police car drove up to the door. The visit was not unexpected. The officer to whom they had talked earlier in the day had promised to make a thorough investigation of the robbery.

Supper was held up while the officers inspected the bungalow, searching for possible clues. They found nothing of interest. Kay and the twins had already gone over the place carefully.

"Do you think the theft was committed by a tramp or someone who happened to be passing and noticed that the door had been left open?" Kay asked one of the men.

"I'd not venture a definite opinion just yet," he

answered. "We've had several robberies in this vicinity recently. Only three nights ago a cottage was broken into down at Harbor Point. This may be the work of the same thief."

Finally the police drove away in their car, and Mrs. Tracey went back to preparing supper. At six o'clock Bill Tracey, who had driven to a nearby town to see a law client, arrived at the cottage and was told of everything that had happened during his absence.

"Well, we could have lost a lot more," he remarked philosophically. "That watch was my old one and never kept good time."

"It was my fault," Kay said apologetically. "I should have locked the door, only we often run down to the beach for a few minutes without closing up the place."

"I've been going to the village and leaving doors open, too," Mrs. Tracey added. "It wasn't your fault, Kay. However, in the future you should be more careful about letting strangers enter the house."

"I've learned my lesson. I felt sorry for Ben, but I don't think he's as innocent as he pretends to be."

After supper Bill worked with his law books and Mrs. Tracey, who had a slight headache, went to her bedroom. Kay and the twins washed the dishes and straightened up the kitchen. Seven-thirty found them without anything to do.

"We might drive over to the Crowley house and make sure that everything is all right there," Kay suggested. "I keep worrying about those two old sisters."

"It will take us only a minute to run over," Betty said eagerly.

The girls told Bill where they were going and then left the house. The storm clouds had disappeared entirely, leaving the air fresh and invigorating. A half moon shone on the sand dunes which dotted the beach as far as one could see.

"It's a beautiful night," Betty remarked as they drove slowly along the road winding through the pine forest. "I could ride like this forever."

"So could I," Wendy added dreamily. Then, reminded of a poem which Lord Byron had written, she began to quote:

> "'There is a pleasure in the pathless wood,
> There is a rapture on the lonely shore,
> There is society where none intrude;
> By the deep sea and music in its roar.'"

She would have recited more of the poem but the Crowley house came into view. Kay stopped the car by the roadside, and as she did the girls noticed a battered automobile parked in a clump of trees not far away. They paid little attention to it as they took the path leading to the house. Suddenly Kay, who was walking slightly ahead of her friends, stopped.

"What's wrong?" Wendy asked instantly.

Kay motioned for the others to be quiet. She moved aside slightly so that they could see the Crowley cottage.

Two men were looking through one of the windows. Inside, a lamp was on. The curtains were open but no one was around in either the kitchen or living room. Apparently the Crowley sisters had left for a few minutes.

The girls were too far away to recognize the intruders. They became thoroughly alarmed as they saw the pair cautiously enter the house.

"They're going to rob those two old ladies!" Kay exclaimed indignantly.

"Maybe it's the same pair who broke into our

cottage!" Betty added. "Shouldn't we get the police?"

"The thieves would be gone before we could bring anyone," Kay told her. She started to move stealthily toward the house.

"We shouldn't do this alone," Wendy said nervously, gripping her friend's hand and trying to stop her. "Those men may be dangerous."

"We can't just stand here while the Crowley sisters are being robbed. At least we can get a look at the thieves so that we can identify them later."

Led by Kay, the three girls quietly made their way to a rear window. Peering cautiously through it, they saw the men working at the doors of the oak cupboard, their backs turned.

"They are thieves!" Kay whispered. "Get out of sight."

As Wendy and Betty ducked, Kay tapped three times on the window pane, then crouched low to avoid being seen. A muffled exclamation came from inside. After a long wait Kay reached up and tapped again on the window, repeating the signal. This time the effect was amazing.

"Ghosts!" they heard one of the men exclaim in fear.

"Ghosts nothing!" the other retorted grimly. "Someone has seen us! Run!"

V

Under Cover of Night

The light inside the Crowley house went out, and two figures darted past the girls. The men ran into the woods, losing themselves among the trees. A moment later a car roared down the road.

"Well, we let them get away," Betty said disgustedly. "I didn't even get a glimpse of their faces."

"Neither did I," Wendy admitted.

It did not occur to the twins that Kay's eyesight might have been better than their own. They were surprised when she said quietly, "I got a pretty good look at them. I'm not absolutely sure, but I think I recognized one."

"Who was he?" Betty asked.

"Ben Wheeler."

"Ben Wheeler," Wendy repeated in amazement. "Oh, I didn't think either of the men looked like him."

"Ben is much taller than those men," Betty added.

"I admit I only got a quick look, but I'm almost certain it was Ben."

"I think you're wrong," Wendy insisted. "I'm sure Betty and I would have recognized Ben."

"But neither of you saw his face."

"That's true," Betty acknowledged, "but both of these men looked short."

"Well, maybe I was wrong," admitted Kay reluctantly. "I wonder where the Crowley sisters are?"

The girls waited by the house for a few minutes. Finally they closed the door which had been left open by the robbers, and after leaving a note for the women, returned to their car. The battered automobile which had been parked in the bushes was gone, proving that it belonged to the prowlers.

"We may as well drive back home," she suggested to her companions. "After the scare we gave them I doubt that they'll return."

As they drove along the winding road, Wendy once more pointed out the sand dunes, but Kay was too occupied with her own thoughts to pay very much attention to what her friend was saying. Suddenly Wendy pointed toward the shore.

"Look over there!" she cried. "What are those two women doing with that shovel?"

Kay instantly braked and turned to stare. Two figures could be seen some distance away, wading up to their ankles in deep sand. One stumbled and fell, then got up with difficulty.

"That looks like Henrietta Crowley!" Kay exclaimed. "And the other is Maud!"

"What are they doing out in the sand dunes at this time of night?" murmured Betty.

Kay parked the car at the side of the road.

"Let's find out," she suggested impulsively. "Maybe they're going to bury the contents of their oak cupboard!"

The Crowley sisters had not noticed the approach of the automobile because they were some distance from the road; nor did they observe Kay and the twins walking stealthily toward them. They stumbled on through the sand dunes. Evidently they were returning home. Henrietta carried the heavy shovel and the girls could hear her breathing hard from the exertion.

"Should we speak to them, Kay?" Betty whispered as the three got closer.

"No, it would frighten them, I think. Let's give them a chance to get home. Can you hear what they're saying?"

The night was unusually still and sound carried well. However, the two women spoke in low tones so that only an occasional phrase reached the ears of the girls. Kay heard the words, "the last of it," while Wendy heard Henrietta say "buried." A moment later they caught the words "from prison."

"What in the world are they talking about?" Betty wondered. "I wish we could get closer."

"That's impossible, unless we want to be seen," Kay told her. "I guess they've buried something, but why they're talking about prison is beyond me."

"Maybe they've stolen something and are afraid they'll be sent to jail for it," said Wendy.

"You have a wild imagination," Betty said, laughing.

The girls waited until the Crowley sisters were out of sight before returning to their car.

"Let's give them plenty of time to get home, and then we'll go back there," Kay suggested.

After fifteen minutes Kay turned the car around and the girls retraced their route. They knocked on the door of the Crowley cottage, but a long time passed before it was opened by Maud. For a moment she stared at them, then her wrinkled face relaxed.

"Oh, it's you! We were frightened for fear it might be prowlers. Someone left a warning note on our doorstep."

"We left it," Kay said. "We just returned to tell you to be sure to lock your doors and windows tonight."

"Why, that's very kind of you but no one will come

here. We have nothing worth stealing. Do step in. Our house isn't very presentable but at least it's cleaner than it was."

The girls came in and accepted the uncomfortable straight-backed chairs which Henrietta offered them. Kay's eyes looked swiftly around the room. Except for the antiques which had been saved from the fire, the place was barren. She believed Maud's declaration— that the Crowley sisters had nothing that would interest a robber.

The girls chatted for several minutes, giving Henrietta and Maud a chance to explain their absence from the house. Henrietta's old-fashioned high-laced shoes had sand on them, yet she offered no explanation. Finally, seeing that both women were tired, Kay and the twins left.

"We didn't learn much," Betty remarked as they returned to the car.

"We learned absolutely nothing," corrected Kay. "Just the same, I think Maud and Henrietta Crowley are involved in some mystery."

"And that means you'll be involved in it soon," Betty said with a chuckle.

"I'd like to find out what it was that they buried in the sand dunes," Kay went on. "Let's see if we can check it out."

"It's pretty late," Wendy protested. "We'd have to go back to the cottage for a shovel, too."

"It is late," Kay agreed. "Maybe it would be better for us to wait until morning. It may take a long time to find whatever is buried there."

The three returned to their cottage, but early the next morning they took a shovel and set out to find what the sisters had hidden. Kay remembered the exact spot where she had seen the Crowley sisters, and found footprints in the sand dunes.

"This will be easy," Betty laughed. "We'll just trace the shoe prints back to the place where the two women were digging."

They followed the trail for a few yards, but were disappointed to find that it suddenly ended. During the night the wind had blown sand around, completely erasing any tracks which had not been partially protected.

"It isn't going to be as simple as I thought," Betty admitted.

"We know the general area where the two women worked last night," Kay nodded, "but without a solid clue we could dig here all day and never find anything."

"Maybe the Crowley sisters marked the spot in some way," Wendy suggested hopefully.

The friends walked on, looking carefully at every likely place. Finally they had to give up and went back to the cottage for a late breakfast.

"I wonder if Ben Wheeler will come today to claim the reward," Mrs. Tracey remarked as she poured coffee.

"If he does, I have a few questions for him," Kay replied. "That boy knows more than he's telling."

She then told her mother and Bill all that she had seen the night before at the Crowley home. They were still talking about it a few minutes later when Betty, who was seated opposite a window, suddenly jumped to her feet.

"There he is now! He's coming up the walk."

"Who?" Kay asked, turning to look out the window.

By that time Ben Wheeler was close to the door. Kay barely had time to tell Bill that she'd rather he didn't say anything that might let Ben know he was under suspicion, when a knock was heard at the kitchen door. Kay went to answer it and with a show of friendliness brought him into the living room. She thought she knew why he had come, but waited for him to speak.

Ben twisted his hat nervously in his hands. "Were you serious about what you said yesterday?" he asked Mrs. Tracey. "Will you give a reward for the return of your stuff?"

"Yes. Have you found any of it?"

Ben grinned and from his trouser pocket took out Bill's watch. Next he put Kay's bracelet on the table.

"Did you find my pearl brooch?" Mrs. Tracey asked eagerly. That was by far the most valuable object which had been taken.

Ben shook his head. "I didn't find any brooch." He seemed to be struggling with himself, then drew a crisp ten-dollar bill from his pocket. "I guess this must be yours, too."

"It could be," Mrs. Tracey answered. "I had one that was new and crisp. The bill looked as if it might have just come from the mint. But I thought it was in a place where no one could find it."

She took the money from Ben and then handed it back to him.

"Keep this as payment for what you have done," she said. Seeing the disappointed look on the boy's face, she added quickly, "If you find the brooch I'll be glad to give you the rest of the reward."

"Where did you find all this?" demanded Bill suspiciously.

"Oh, just around the waterfront," he answered vaguely, backing toward the door.

"Not in the woods?" Kay asked before he could escape.

"No, I looked there but I didn't find anything. I had a terrible time finding the stuff, and I nearly got killed."

"You nearly got killed?" Mrs. Tracey repeated in amazement, not knowing whether to believe him.

"You mean the thief nearly caught you?" Kay asked.

"Almost," Ben answered uneasily.

Again he tried to retreat. Without being obvious about it Kay blocked the door.

"Where did you find the jewelry, Ben?" she asked. "Tell us."

"The things were on a boat," he replied reluctantly. "A river boat," he added, evading Kay's eyes. "I'm in a hurry—I've got to leave now."

Kay smiled.

"Of course," she said evenly. "We wouldn't think of delaying you. But before you go, tell us the name of the boat."

VI

A Sealed Bottle

Ben Wheeler found the question an embarrassing one. He hesitated, then gave his answer without looking directly at Kay.

"I guess it was the *Rover*."

"You guess!" exclaimed Bill sharply. He was certain the boy was lying. "Aren't you sure?"

"It was the *Rover*, for sure," Ben muttered, moving away. "I have to go now."

Kay stepped aside to let him pass. He left the house and disappeared from view down the beach.

"That boy should be turned over to the police and locked up!" Bill said angrily. "I never saw such nerve! He robs the house, then returns our things and claims a reward!"

"It looks that way," agreed Kay. "I'm sure he wasn't telling the truth about the name of the boat, but I'm going to check up on his story."

"Well, at least we have some of our things back, and that's something," said Mrs. Tracey cheerfully. "I never expected to see any of them again."

She insisted on returning ten dollars to Wendy to compensate for the money she had lost. Then the group returned to breakfast.

It was another cold, bleak day with a fine mist drizzling down on the sand. "Fine weather we're having," Betty grumbled, her nose pressed against a window.

"Cheer up," said Kay, "there are plenty of new magazines. Look, here's the one with all the new back-to-school clothes."

So the girls spent a quiet day, sitting close to the fire, reading and talking to Mrs. Tracey. Just before dusk, Kay became restless.

"Mist is letting up," she announced, coming back from the front porch. "Let's take a walk up the beach and get some fresh air."

Wendy and Betty were happy to get out and the three ran off to get jackets and scarves.

"Don't stay out too long, girls," Mrs. Tracey warned. "It might start to rain, and the tide is going to be high in an hour. I wouldn't want you marooned on some sandbar."

"We'll be right back," Kay assured her.

The trio walked briskly down the shoreline, glad to feel the moist, cold wind against their faces.

"I didn't realize how groggy I was getting," said Wendy after a few minutes.

Suddenly the three stopped. Far out over the ocean they could see a blue ball of light tumbling down the horizon.

"Falling star," said Betty. "Make a wish."

"That's not a star, Betty," answered Kay. "It went up before it came down. Let's see if there's another one."

Minutes passed. A second streak of light did not appear. Just as they were about to turn and go home, the blue flare shone again.

"What is it, Kay?" Wendy asked.

"It's a distress rocket. Maybe from a boat or a plane out in the ocean. Come on, we'd better notify the Coast Guard!"

With Kay in the lead, the three ran back to the cottage. Breathlessly Kay explained to her mother what they had seen. Since there was no phone in the cottage, Mrs. Tracey handed her the keys to the car.

In a matter of minutes, Kay, Betty and Wendy were climbing the steps of the Coast Guard station.

"May I speak to the man in charge here?" Kay asked the curly-haired guardsman who answered her knock.

In a few minutes, Kay had told her story to the lieutenant in command of the station. He took down everything the girls could remember about the blue flashes.

"Hmm, must be fairly close to land. I'll try to pick it up on our radar screen. Meantime, I'll contact the nearest cutter, and send it to the area right away. We'll let you know as soon as we find out anything, Miss Tracey."

All the way back along the lonely shore road, the girls kept looking out to sea. No more flares appeared. It was a dark night, with heavy clouds hiding the moon and stars.

"Think of tossing around out there in the dark, all alone," murmured Wendy, adding,

"The wild sea sings a sad refrain,
Sailors, you'll never see home again."

"Wendy," her twin interrupted, "do you have to be so gloomy? I know it's supposed to be poetic and all that, but give me a break."

"Let's get home and turn on the local radio station," Kay suggested. "It'll probably have whatever news there is."

Back at the cottage, they sat down to a late supper. They ate without talking, listening intently for a news bulletin. A disc jockey was playing the week's top hits when the bulletin came on.

"The Coast Guard is investigating reports of distress flares seen late this afternoon off the beach near the cottage colony. The Harbor Point airport reports that a plane piloted by Jack Breen is two hours overdue. When last heard from, Breen radioed that his starboard engine had failed. He said he thought he could make the remaining distance on one engine, but since that time there has been no word from the famous pilot. Stay tuned to this station for further developments."

"Jack Breen!" Kay exclaimed. "Why he's one of the most famous pilots in the country. I wonder why he was coming to Harbor Point."

"How exciting!" Betty cried. "He's so handsome. There was a picture of him in last week's paper when he got back from that trip over the South American jungles."

As the girls were finishing the dishes, Bill came in. Talking all at once, the twins and Kay told him about the evening's happenings.

"Hey," he practically shouted, putting his hands over his ears, "one, maybe even two I could listen to, but not the three of you."

"It's Kay's story," Betty said. "Let her tell it."

So Kay described once more the walk along the beach, the flares, and the trip to the Coast Guard. Just as she finished, the radio broadcasted another news bulletin.

"A Coast Guard cutter has picked up Jack Breen, the famous pilot whose plane crashed at sea a few hours ago. Breen is unhurt, but was unable to make contact with the shore because his emergency radio transmitter was lost when a wave swamped his rubber raft. Credit for his prompt rescue goes to Miss Kay Tracey of Brantwood, who is spending the summer at the beach.

On a walk with two friends, Miss Tracey saw flares sent up by Mr. Breen and quickly reported them to the Coast Guard station."

"Well, that's good news," said Kay, falling into a chair with a sigh of relief. "I couldn't have slept tonight without some definite news."

At ten o'clock everyone went to bed, and things were quiet for the night. Kay slept soundly until toward midnight, when in the midst of a pleasant dream she was suddenly awakened.

Someone was knocking on the door of the cottage!

For a minute Kay lay still, listening. In her drowsy state she thought that the thief who had robbed the cottage might have returned. Then she gave up that idea, realizing that a prowler would not advertise his arrival.

No one else in the house seemed to have heard the knock. As Kay waited, it was repeated.

"I'll have to go downstairs," she decided, reluctantly leaving her warm bed. "I wonder who would come here at this time of night?"

VII

A Messenger

Before switching on the lights in the living room, Kay peered out the window to see who was standing at the door. She was somewhat reassured to see a man in uniform.

"Who can that be? Maybe it's one of the police checking to see if there have been any more thefts," Kay thought.

Opening the door, she found the late visitor was the lieutenant from the Coast Guard station.

"Sorry to bother you so late, Miss Tracey," he said, "but I'm off duty and on my way home. I wanted to let you know firsthand that Breen is safe. They're checking him thoroughly in the hospital, and he'll stay there tonight, but I'm sure he'll be out tomorrow."

"I'm glad to hear that," Kay said gratefully. "Won't you come in?"

"No, thank you," the young man answered. "This rescue has made me late as it is, and I better not lose any more time. I just wanted to tell you how much we all appreciate your help."

The lieutenant threw Kay a salute and turned away into the night.

"Kay dear, who's that at the door?" Mrs. Tracey called from the stairway.

Her daughter told her, adding, "I wonder why Breen happened to come here. It's such a small, out-of-the-way place, and very few people know about it."

Mrs. Tracey glanced at the clock, and Kay turned toward the stairway. At that moment they heard a slight scraping sound outside the door.

"What was that?" Kay asked in a low voice.

Scarcely had she spoken, when someone knocked on the door. After a brief hesitation Mrs. Tracey went to see who was standing outside.

"Ben Wheeler!" she exclaimed as she peered out into the darkness. "What brings you here so late at night?"

"I saw your light," the boy answered apologetically. "I thought you were still up, or I wouldn't have rapped."

"What is it you want?"

"I've found the rest of your stolen jewelry, Mrs. Tracey."

Ben took from his pocket the pearl brooch and a number of inexpensive articles, several of which Kay and the twins had not even missed.

"And now may I have the rest of the reward?" the boy asked eagerly as Mrs. Tracey examined the brooch.

"Yes, step inside a minute, Ben. I'll get you the money."

While her mother was in another room, Kay tried to get Ben into a conversation but he was more cautious than he had been before.

"You're amazing when it comes to finding things," she said flatteringly. "Did you find these things on the *Rover* too?"

"That's right," Ben mumbled, lowering his eyes.

"You risked your life to make a return trip? I'm surprised that the thieves weren't on the lookout for you."

Ben offered no reply. Mrs. Tracey came back with

the money she had promised him. With a muttered
"Thanks" he quickly left the house.

"We'll probably never see him again," Mrs. Tracey
commented as she turned out the lights. "However, I
think your first guess was right, Kay. He more than
likely is the thief who took our things."

"Unfortunately there's no way to prove anything
against him, Mother."

"No, we may as well forget the entire affair. Let's
go to bed before we wake up everyone else."

While Kay and the twins were eating breakfast the
next morning, Jack Breen came to the cottage. He was
just as handsome as his pictures.

"I don't know how to thank you properly," he told
Kay, "but I do have this trinket with me. It was in my
jacket pocket. I've been carrying it since I returned
from South America. An Indian friend made it."

Jack Breen handed Kay a bracelet of dark,
polished wood, hand-carved with intricate figures.

"Now," he continued, "I wonder if you would do a
favor for me. I am looking for the Crowley sisters. They
were my reason for the trip to this place. Do you know
where they live?"

"Oh," said Kay, "you know them?"

"No," Jack Breen replied, "but I have news for
them that only I can take them."

Kay gave him directions for reaching the cottage
of the eccentric women. She wished she could question
him more, but did not dare intrude. After pleasant
good-byes, the pilot left, walking off in the direction of
the Crowley house.

It was a beautiful sunny day, and the twins and
Kay soon forgot the worry of the night before,
swimming and sunning on the beach.

They were having so much fun that Kay pushed
the mystery of the Crowley sisters out of her mind. But

she was too intrigued to forget it for very long, and next day found an excuse to visit them again.

"I have an idea!" Kay exclaimed. "Let's bake a cake and some cookies for the Crowley sisters. I don't believe they have even enough to eat."

"I'm sure they don't," Wendy added. "When we were there I looked in the kitchen cupboards and they were practically empty."

The girls made butterscotch cookies and a large chocolate cake with thick frosting.

"I hope the Crowley sisters won't be offended by our offering them food," Kay said as they started for the house. "You never can tell how they'll react. They're so proud."

A surprise awaited the girls at the cottage. The door stood open but the women were not at home. Mr. Peter Wake was the sole occupant of the place.

"Good morning," he greeted Kay and the twins pleasantly.

"We have a gift for the Crowleys," Kay said politely. "Are they at home?"

The man shook his head.

"Can you tell me when they'll be back?"

"They will not be back at all," Mr. Wake answered. "Early this morning they left for New York where they plan to live with relatives."

Kay stared at the man in surprise.

"That's strange," she murmured. "Henrietta and Maud Crowley never spoke about any relatives. I thought that they were alone in the world."

"What will be done with their things?" Wendy inquired curiously.

"Oh, I'm in charge here," Mr. Wake replied quickly. "I'll look after everything. You see, for months I've been trying to get the sisters to leave this house.

During the past year they've been practically penniless, but they'd rather starve than accept help."

"But now they've decided to live with relatives?" questioned Kay.

"Well, that's not exactly true," Mr. Wake admitted after a slight hesitation. "I only told you that because Henrietta and Maud want people to believe it."

"They've gone to a retirement home?" Kay guessed.

"Yes, it was the only thing they could do. This home isn't half bad. It's privately run. In return for their furniture I'm taking care of the small expense of establishing them there."

"The furniture is really beautiful, isn't it?" Kay said, glancing about.

"Yes, most of the pieces are genuine antiques. You can't pick up stuff like this every day of the week. I am adding all of it to my private collection."

"Where is the retirement home?" Kay asked.

"Not far from New York City. The Crowley sisters want their neighbors to believe that they are living with relatives."

"We'll never tell anyone," Betty assured him. "I feel sorry for them having to go away. They loved this cottage, and they're so proud."

"Yes," Mr. Wake acknowledged, "it is hard for them. But what else is there to do? They are absolutely without funds. As I said, I tried for months to persuade them to leave. You know, I suspect they have a special reason for wanting to stay here."

"A reason besides their love for the house?" Kay asked.

"Yes, I think they have an attachment to the place which has to do with some secret connected with it."

"We noticed that too," said Kay. "For one thing,

they seemed to be afraid that someone would find out what was in their oak cupboard."

"Shall we have a look at it?" Mr. Wake suggested. "I had just started to look around when you girls arrived."

Now that the two women had gone away, Kay and the twins thought it would be all right for them to investigate the cupboard. The doors opened easily at Mr. Wake's touch. Inside were a basket of sewing materials, a few books, and several choice dishes. Mr. Wake immediately turned his attention to the antiques, forgetting his original intention.

"If anything valuable ever was kept here, it's gone now," Wendy remarked.

"Don't you consider this teapot valuable?" Mr. Wake demanded. "Perhaps it wouldn't bring ten dollars at a sale, but actually such china can't be bought except from private owners. When people learn to appreciate dishes such as these, prices will soar out of sight."

While Mr. Wake admired his discoveries, Kay and the twins wandered around the house searching for possible hiding places. They found nothing of interest.

"I'll bet the Crowley sisters hid their treasure before they went away," Kay said finally. "It's probably buried somewhere in the sand dunes."

"No one will ever find it then," Wendy added gloomily. "In a few weeks the wind will shift the sand, all landmarks will be erased, and then the two sisters themselves won't have the faintest idea where they hid their treasure."

Kay nodded and crossed the room to talk with Mr. Wake again. She thought she should tell him about the robberies which had been committed in the neighborhood recently.

"I hope you plan to move out the furniture soon,"

she said. "With the house closed up I wouldn't consider it very safe here."

Mr. Wake was grateful for the information. He had intended to leave the house as it was for at least a week.

"This changes all my plans," he declared. "I can't risk having any of this furniture stolen. I've got to get it out right away. Unfortunately, I have to go to the city on business and I'll be gone nearly all day. How will I find a reliable mover?"

"Maybe we could help," Kay offered impulsively. "I think my cousin knows a reliable man in the village."

Mr. Wake was very pleased with Kay's offer and quickly accepted it. After leaving careful instructions about moving the furniture, he gave the key of the house to her and quickly drove away.

"You've gotten yourself into a nice job now, Kay," Betty remarked when they were alone.

"Yes, I guess I have, but we've got nothing special to do today. I really don't mind."

"Neither do we," Betty said quickly. "I wanted to go to town anyway."

Returning to the Tracey cottage, the girls hailed Bill just as he was leaving. He told them the name of a reliable moving company, and they went off immediately to make arrangements for moving the Crowley furniture.

"I hate to think of those two nice people spending their last days in an institution," Kay said as they drove along. "They must feel humiliated."

"I bet it was hard for them to leave," Wendy added. "It makes me think of the poem,

> "'Old papers thrown away,
> Old garments cast aside,
> The talk of yesterday,

> Are things identified;
> But time once torn away
> No voice can recall.'"

"The Crowleys had so many happy memories of their home," said Betty.

"And maybe a few unhappy ones, too," Kay added.

"What makes you say that?" Wendy asked quickly.

"Oh, I thought they seemed sort of sad. Maybe it was because they knew the time was coming when they'd have to go away, but I always thought they had some sad secret."

They had reached the village, and Kay drove to the office of a moving company. She arranged for a van to come to the Crowley house right away and the girls led the way in their car. Suddenly Kay began to laugh, and the twins looked at her in amazement.

"Now that the Crowleys have gone and Mr. Wake is leaving, there's no reason why we can't try everything to solve the secret of the sand dunes," she announced. "And we can start today!"

VIII

Souvenirs

"Hey, I'm not going to drive my van through all that loose sand," the driver of the furniture truck protested when the two cars reached the turn from the main road. "I might get stuck."

"It's only a short distance from here to the Crowley house," Kay told the man. "I've often seen delivery trucks come in here." It took a lot of argument to convince him but he finally agreed to drive on.

The girls opened up the Crowley cottage and directed the men handling the fragile pieces of furniture. Sweeping the floor of the living room after it had been cleared, Kay found several old-fashioned black jet buttons.

"Aren't these strange?" she asked Wendy. "You hardly ever see buttons like these any more. They must have come from the sisters' clothes."

"Some people collect old buttons, Kay. Why don't you keep one as a souvenir?"

"I think I will," her friend decided after a little hesitation.

A few minutes later, while emptying the contents of a drawer, Betty found an elbow-length glove which had no mate.

"Do you think anyone would care if I took it?" she asked the others.

"I doubt it," answered Kay.

"I'm the only one who doesn't have a souvenir," Wendy complained. "I wish I could find something."

"Here, you can have this," Kay smiled, picking up something from the floor. It was a large gold hairpin.

The van was nearly loaded by this time, and the driver came to ask where the furniture was to be taken.

"Mr. Wake said he'd return for a few minutes before the truck leaves," Kay answered. "I think he wants the things taken to his own home but I'm not sure."

To everyone's relief Mr. Wake drove up just as the last piece of furniture was being lifted into the van. He talked with the driver for a minute or two and then came to talk with the girls.

"I can't tell you how grateful I am for your help," he told them. "I never could have managed otherwise."

"Everything is out of the house now," Kay assured him. "And here is the key."

"Allow me to pay you for your work."

"Oh, no," Kay protested, "but we are taking these small trinkets if you don't mind."

The girls displayed the gold hairpin, the button, and the glove.

"By all means keep them. They're not important." Mr. Wake glanced at his watch. "I must hurry if I am to reach the city before noon. Again, thank you." He lifted his hat and walked to his car.

By the time the girls went to their own car a few minutes later the truck was out of sight. Not until then did Betty ask where the furniture had been taken.

"I guess to Mr. Wake's home," Wendy replied. "I saw him give instructions to the driver. Do you know where Mr. Wake lives, Kay?"

"No, I don't. I meant to ask him but he went away so quickly it slipped my mind."

"We'll probably meet him again after he returns from his business trip," said Betty.

"The furniture isn't our problem now that it's out of our hands," Kay added. "I'm more interested in finding what was buried by the Crowley sisters."

"I wish we could dig it up," Wendy said eagerly.

"Maybe we can," Kay replied. "Our vacation doesn't end for a while and we'll have time to search the sand dunes."

The girls drove slowly back to the cottage, having no idea that it was long past lunchtime. Kay was surprised to find the front door locked, but the key had been left under a mat.

"Mother doesn't seem to be here," she said, unlocking the door.

The house was deserted. In the kitchen the girls found their lunch steaming on the stove, but there was no note from Mrs. Tracey.

"I wonder where she could have gone?" Kay said anxiously. "She didn't have the car so she must have walked."

"It's after two o'clock," Betty pointed out, glancing at a clock.

"You eat your lunch," Kay said. "I think I'll see if I can find my mother."

"No, we'll go with you," insisted Betty. "I'm not hungry anyway."

Despite Kay's protests, the twins would not let her leave without them. The three set off on foot, sure that Mrs. Tracey would be somewhere along the beach. It didn't occur to them that she might have gotten worried over their long absence and gone to look for them. Actually, Mrs. Tracey had waited until Bill had come home for lunch, and then together they had taken his car and driven to the Crowley house. They had taken a different route than the one taken by the girls, and the two cars had not passed each other.

A short distance down the beach Kay and the twins met a stout woman in a tailored tweed suit. She was walking along briskly. She stared at the girls with a curious, penetrating gaze, then turned her head away, and continued on, but Kay stopped her.

"I beg your pardon," Kay said quickly.

"Yes?" the woman inquired, halting.

"I'm looking for my mother and I thought you might have seen her farther down the beach. She's in her forties, and is probably wearing a blue felt hat and blue coat."

"I haven't seen anyone on the beach this afternoon. Has she been missing long?"

"I'm not sure. The house was empty when we came back a few minutes ago. It's not like her to go away without leaving a note. I wouldn't be worried, only our house was robbed the other night and I've heard that some suspicious looking people have been seen in the area."

"Well, maybe I can help you," the woman said, her stern face relaxing into a smile. "It happens that finding missing persons is my job."

"You're not a detective!"

"Not exactly, but I do a great deal of investigation work. I'm a policewoman." Opening her coat, she displayed an inconspicuous badge which she wore on her blouse.

"Your life must be really exciting," exclaimed Kay enviously.

"Sometimes, but in general the work of our department is more or less routine. My name is Jane Vernon and I'm from Denver."

"Are you here on a case?" Kay asked, hoping that

the woman would reveal more about herself.

"No, my sister and I are here on vacation—precious few I ever get! But now, I'm rattling on about myself and not helping you a bit. Tell me about the robbery, and give me a more detailed description of your mother. I never forget a face."

Kay gave her the information, and Mrs. Vernon promised that she would keep an eye out for Mrs. Tracey.

"I'd love to hear more about your work," Betty said eagerly as the girls turned away.

"Come to my cottage any time," the policewoman invited cordially. "It's lonesome for my sister without visitors. She'll be glad to meet you."

Mrs. Vernon scribbled an address on one of her cards and gave it to Kay.

"She's nice, even if she is a bit blunt and kind of tough looking," Betty said to Kay and Wendy when the woman was out of earshot. "I'd like to have a long talk with her some time."

Convinced that Mrs. Tracey was not on the beach, the three walked back toward the road. They had gone only a short distance when they saw Ben Wheeler slouching toward them. He would have turned aside to avoid meeting them, if Kay hadn't called his name.

"Oh, Ben!"

"Yes?" Reluctantly he stopped and waited for the girls.

"I'm looking for my mother," Kay explained. "Have you seen—what's the matter with your eye? And your hands are all bruised. Were you in a fight?"

"Maybe."

"You don't look very cheerful," Wendy observed. "I guess you must have gotten the worst of it."

Ben did not answer. It was obvious that he had no

intention of offering any information about himself.

"A person can get pretty discouraged sometimes," he muttered, his eyes fixed on the ground. "If I just had some money——"

"Have you lost the twenty-five dollars my mother gave you?" asked Kay.

"I need more than that. I need at least ten dollars more—I have to get it."

"Are you saving your money for some particular reason?" Kay inquired.

"That's right." Ben's voice was eager. "Say, could you lend me a few dollars? I'll pay you back in a week or two. Honest I will. I wouldn't ask, only I really need it."

"I don't have a penny with me," Kay replied truthfully. "I left my bag at the cottage."

Ben looked hopefully at Wendy and Betty, but the twins shook their heads.

"Then I guess I'm out of luck," Ben said gloomily. "I don't know what I'll do."

"Why do you need the money so desperately?" Kay inquired.

Before Ben could answer, a car came down the road.

"There's your mother now!" cried Betty.

Forgetting Ben, the girls ran to the roadside. Bill had seen them and had brought the car to a stop.

"So here you are!" he greeted the trio. "We've toured six states looking for you. Where have you been, anyway?"

"Looking for Mother," Kay laughed. "First we helped Mr. Wake move the Crowley furniture. Then, when we came home, the place was deserted."

"We were out looking for you," Mrs. Tracey explained. "I couldn't imagine what had delayed you. You're almost never late for lunch."

"We forgot all about it," admitted Kay. "So many things happened at the Crowley cottage. Did you know that the sisters are gone?"

"Gone!" Mrs. Tracey exclaimed. "Why, no! Bill and I noticed that the house looked deserted but we thought they had simply gone away for a few hours."

Kay told them about the arrangement which had been made between Mr. Wake and the two women.

"If they're penniless I suppose they had no choice," Mrs. Tracey remarked. "But it does seem a pity!"

"Let's get back to the cottage," Bill suggested, opening the car door. "Lunch has been waiting an hour and I'm starved."

Kay hesitated, but did not follow the twins into the car.

"Oh, Bill," she said apologetically, "could you lend me some money—about ten dollars?"

"Kay," Mrs. Tracey interposed, "what do you need it for?"

"It's not for me. We just met Ben Wheeler and he told us he needed it desperately."

"Ben Wheeler!" said Bill contemptuously. "You're being taken in by that kid. I don't trust him at all."

"I guess it would be stupid to lend him money," Kay admitted as she opened the car door. "Only he acted as if he really needs it."

Bill opened his wallet and took out two five-dollar bills which he offered to Kay.

"Thanks a million," Kay smiled gratefully. "I'll pay it back."

Kay ran down the beach to find Ben. Soon she returned to the car, disappointed.

"I couldn't find him," she reported, giving the money back to Bill. "He seems to have disappeared."

IX

Kay Investigates

"I've noticed Ben Wheeler has a habit of disappearing," Bill commented dryly as Kay climbed into the car beside him.

"But this time he had no reason to run away," Kay replied, her eyes on the road. "I can't figure him out."

"You worry about him too much," Mrs. Tracey scolded Kay. "Now that we've gotten back our stolen property, I prefer to forget the entire matter."

"I can't forget it, Mother. I keep wondering if Ben is guilty or innocent."

"He's probably guilty," Bill assured her. "I've seen plenty of kids like him brought into juvenile court."

"You can't judge a person entirely by his appearance, Bill."

"Circumstantial evidence is against him, Kay. But he's smart enough to keep from getting caught."

Kay dropped the subject. She knew that her mother didn't want to hear any more about it. During the ride home, Kay lapsed into silence. She saw the truth in what Bill said and respected his judgment. His legal practice brought him into contact with many juvenile offenders. Kay distrusted Ben, but she thought that he had some good points that might develop if someone took an interest in his welfare.

After lunch at the cottage, everyone was surprised

when a police officer came by. Sergeant Kelley had been assigned to the robbery case.

"That's good," Bill responded. "Have you found the thief yet?"

"I expect to make an arrest before the end of the day," Kelley answered.

At this unexpected remark Kay, who had only been half listening, became very interested.

"You sure worked quickly, Sergeant Kelley," she said. "There were so few clues, I didn't think it would be possible to prove a case. Who's the suspect?"

"A fisherman by the name of Henry Swope. He and his family live in a shack down by the docks."

"Why do you suspect him?" asked Mrs. Tracey in a puzzled tone.

"Well, in the first place, Swope has no visible means of support."

"But you said he was a fisherman," Bill interposed.

"Oh, sure, but he doesn't make very much."

"Has he any children?" Mrs. Tracey asked.

"Six, ma'am. They're all under eleven years of age. And that's just the point. He's had a hard time making ends meet up until this week. Now he's wearing new clothes, and buying new furniture for his shack. Nothing cheap, mind you—a six-hundred-dollar sofa and things like that."

"We didn't lose six hundred dollars," Kay remarked dryly, "so Mr. Swope couldn't have stolen the money from us."

"A half dozen robberies have been reported in the past two weeks," Sergeant Kelley continued. "Swope began to show off his money just about that time. We're watching him."

"I'd move slowly," Bill advised. "We wouldn't want to press charges unless the evidence against the man was conclusive."

"Don't worry! That's the only kind of evidence I get," Sergeant Kelley said, boasting. He turned toward the door. "Well, I must be going. You'll hear from me after I've made an arrest."

"Mr. Kelley," Kay said quickly, "did you say the Swopes live down by the docks?"

"That's right, Miss. On Fulton Street. Their place is the next to the last one on the north side."

"I'd like to talk with Mr. Swope. Do you mind, Mother?"

"I wish you would, dear; that is, if Sergeant Kelley doesn't mind."

"I can't see what good you can do, Miss," the policeman responded, "but you're welcome to come along with me if you like. I'm on my way down there now."

As they walked toward the docks, Sergeant Kelley told Kay what little he knew about Henry Swope and his wife, Ida. The couple was not well known in the area, even though Swope had been born at Seaside Beach. He had moved away from the community years before and had returned only eight months ago.

"Swope doesn't let people find out much about his past," Kelley said. "When I try to question him he shuts up like a clam."

"That's not surprising, is it, if he knows he is under suspicion?"

"I'll make him talk today. If he doesn't I'll run him in!"

"Has he ever been in trouble before this?" Kay asked as they turned into a narrow dirty street close to the waterfront.

"Not as far as anyone can find out. But he's tricky."

Groups of ragged children stopped playing and stared at Kay and the policeman. A tired looking woman of thirty-eight or so, her hair straggling over her eyes, her house dress wrinkled but clean, emerged from one of the tumbledown shacks, a crying baby in her arms.

"That's Mrs. Swope," Kelley indicated.

The woman saw the pair, and guessing their purpose, she darted back inside and closed the door. A moment later when the policeman knocked there was no answer.

"Open up!" Kelley shouted angrily. "Open the door!"

After a long wait one of the living room windows was pushed up. Mrs. Swope peered out, her face distorted with fear.

"What do you want?" she asked defensively. "If you're after Henry, he ain't here."

"Open the door!" Kelley commanded.

Kay did not like the sergeant's attitude. She thought that he would gain nothing by badgering the woman.

"Please let us in," Kay said politely. "We're not here to make trouble for your husband."

Mrs. Swope seemed uncertain at this abrupt change of tactics, but after a moment of hesitation she did unlock the door.

Kay stepped into a very messy room. There was very little furniture, yet it appeared to be cluttered because papers, toys, and children's clothes were scattered everywhere. A boy and a girl of five, obviously twins, had been playing with blocks in one corner of the room. Now they huddled in fear against a wall. In the kitchen she saw an older girl of about ten washing clothes over a steaming tub. The child in Mrs. Swope's arms screamed loudly despite the woman's efforts to quiet it.

"Where's your husband?" Sergeant Kelley demanded irritably.

"I told you he ain't here," the woman answered sullenly. "He's looking after his nets."

The policeman's gaze traveled around the room. "What became of that sofa you had here yesterday?" he demanded. "And the radio?"

"We gave them to a man for a grocery bill we'd been owing for over six months," Mrs. Swope replied defiantly. "Why do you always come here snooping around? My husband is good and honest. He never did anything wrong!"

"We don't want to make trouble for him," Kay said.

"The police keep hounding us all the time. They say my husband stole money but it's not true! Our new furniture was given to us by a relative. But the bill collectors wouldn't let us keep it!"

"I believe you," Kay said sympathetically.

Sergeant Kelley scowled at her. "I won't get anywhere with you siding in with the Swopes," he muttered irritably. "I'm leaving!"

Kay was not sorry to see him leave. After the door slammed behind him she gained Mrs. Swope's confidence by asking her questions about the children. The baby stopped crying and was allowed to creep on the floor.

"He's a cute baby," Kay declared, "but isn't he a little underweight?"

"Three pounds," Mrs. Swope admitted. "We don't have enough money to buy the food Jackie needs. My husband is a hard working man but in these times he can't make ends meet."

Kay decided that as soon as she left she would stop at a grocery store and have some food delivered to Mrs. Swope. Even if it were true that her husband had stolen money, his family should be helped. As Kay talked with the woman, hoping to learn something of her past, she became aware of the odor of cooking.

"It smells like something's burning, Mrs. Swope."

"My bread!" the woman cried, and ran out of the room.

Smoke came out of the oven as she opened it, but only the tops of two loaves had gotten too brown. Mrs. Swope lifted out the bread, put it on a table, and rubbed margarine over the loaves.

"If you hadn't smelled it I'd have lost it all," she said gratefully to Kay. "I don't know what I'd have done. I've used the last of my flour."

"Can't you borrow money from your relatives?" Kay suggested, watching the woman's face closely.

"They wouldn't give us a penny—not them."

"But they gave you a sofa and a radio."

"Things they didn't want in their own house. I've written to my husband's sister time after time, but the only help she ever gave us was to send the furniture. The bill collectors took it away almost as soon as we got it in the house."

Kay now directed the conversation toward the Crowley sisters.

"Why, I know them," the woman declared. "Last Christmas they brought toys for the children. Folks say they haven't much money, but they're good and kind and willing to share what little they have with others."

"Yes, I'm sure that's true, Mrs. Swope. They've gone away for a while, I believe."

"Have they closed up their house?" Mrs. Swope asked in surprise. "I never thought they'd leave it."

"I wonder why they seemed so attached to the place? It wasn't very comfortable."

"People tell me their brother used to live with them. He was a sailor and one day he disappeared. I guess they've kept watching for him all these years, hoping he'd come back."

"I didn't know that the Crowley sisters had a brother. Was he lost at sea?"

"I never did hear the details, Miss. But I take it that's why the two sisters wanted to stay on in the house."

"You think that's the only reason?" Kay probed, wondering if Mrs. Swope had heard gossip regarding the oak cupboard.

"Old people always get attached to a place."

Kay was convinced that Mrs. Swope didn't suspect there was any secret guarded by the old women. While the two were talking, Mr. Swope, a stoop-shouldered man with prematurely gray hair, entered the house. He glanced a little suspiciously at Kay, but his wife introduced her as a friend.

"She's here to help us, Henry. The police came again today and——"

"What right have they breaking into our home?" the fisherman demanded angrily. "Just because I'm hard up they try to lay a crime on me! Why, I never stole a penny in my life!"

"I'm sure you never did," said Kay.

"Can they arrest me for something I didn't do?"

"Not without evidence. Do you remember where you were the night of the storm?"

"Right here all afternoon and evening. I had to lay in all day on account of the weather."

"Did anyone besides your wife and children see you here at your home?"

"None that I know of. But wait. Jerry Cranshaw dropped in after supper, come to think about it."

"That would be too late to establish your alibi for the robbery," said Kay regretfully. "But don't worry, Mr. Swope. I'm sure the police won't arrest you."

"Just let 'em try. I'll be ready for them next time they come busting in here."

"If you take that attitude you'll be almost sure to end up in jail," Kay warned him. "Try to be polite to the police, answer their questions, and tell them the exact truth. They won't be so hostile if you do that."

"Maybe there's something in what you say," Mr. Swope admitted reluctantly.

When Kay was ready to leave a few minutes later, Mr. Swope insisted on giving her some fresh fish which he had caught that day. She accepted his gift and to ease her conscience for taking the food, she stopped at the nearest grocery store and ordered a long list of items to be sent to the Swopes. She did not want to include her name so she told the owner to say that it had been sent by a friend.

"I wonder what Bill will think when he hears about this?" Kay thought cheerfully. "He'll probably decide I'm very softhearted. But I bet he would do the same thing. Mr. Swope doesn't look like a thief and I'm certain he had nothing to do with the robbery."

As Kay approached her own cottage, a few minutes later, she met Ben Wheeler. She stopped, expecting him to ask for money again. He seemed very depressed, and did not have much to say.

"How would you like a fish for your dinner?" Kay asked, taking a large one from her bag. "I have more than I'll be able to use."

"Thanks," Ben responded in pleased surprise. "Sure, I'd like to have it."

As Kay started to move on again, he stopped her.

"There's something I want to say—" he began nervously.

"Yes."

"I—I don't know what you think of me, but I'm not as bad as I seem. You've been real nice to me. Maybe some day I'll be able to repay you."

Kay stood looking at him for a moment. Then she

said quietly, "Ben, I don't know what you have done or the trouble you may be in, but why don't you give up being a beachcomber and go back west?"

"If only I could!"

"I'll pay your fare."

He shook his head. "It's not a case of money," he said, averting his eyes. "You don't understand."

"Maybe I could."

A frightened expression came into the boy's face. "I can never go home now," he said brokenly. "There's this guy I can't get away from."

Before Kay could ask one question Ben turned and ran into the woods.

X

Trailing the *Rover*

Kay continued toward the cottage, troubled by what Ben had said. She could interpret his words in only one way. Obviously he was involved with a criminal.

"He probably did have a part in the robbery," she reflected. "I wish he hadn't run away. He must have been afraid I would learn too much."

Mrs. Tracey and the Worth twins were eagerly waiting for Kay. They listened to her account of what happened at the Swope home, and agreed that the evidence against the fisherman was too slight to justify the police taking action against him.

"The fish are cleaned," Mrs. Tracey remarked as she peered into Kay's bag. "I'll bake this large one for dinner tonight."

At six o'clock Bill came home in an unusually happy mood. He went for a brief swim with Kay and the twins, tormenting them by swimming under water and pulling them under.

Mrs. Tracey had made an unusually good dinner. The fish was excellent and Bill ate far more than his share. Suddenly he began to cough and choke.

"Drink some water," Mrs. Tracey advised anxiously. "You must have swallowed a bone."

Bill removed a small object from his mouth.

"Well, look what I've found!" he exclaimed. "A ring!"

"It is!" Kay exclaimed in amazement. "How did it ever get inside the fish?"

"I didn't notice it when I stuffed the fish," Mrs. Tracey protested. "I washed it carefully, too."

"Do you think that blue stone is valuable?" Wendy asked eagerly. "Once a friend of mine found a large pearl in an oyster and it was worth one hundred dollars."

"This looks like a woman's ring," Bill said. "Maybe someone dropped it from an ocean liner and this fish just snapped it up!"

"A very interesting theory," said Kay. "Let me see it, Bill."

"If you ask very nicely I might be persuaded to give it to you as a gift."

"That's very kind of you, Bill. But I don't wear rings that come as prizes in popcorn boxes!"

"Popcorn!" Betty cried.

"Don't you remember that box we bought three nights ago?" Kay asked, laughing. "This is the ring that was inside. Bill is playing a joke on us!"

"The fish never swallowed it at all?" Wendy asked.

"Of course not," Kay replied. "Mother would have noticed the ring when she made the fish. Bill just stuck it in his mouth when we weren't looking."

"I can never fool Kay," Bill complained good-naturedly. "But I had her excited for a minute."

Mrs. Tracey and the girls cleared away the dishes while Bill settled himself in a comfortable chair to read the evening newspaper. When Kay returned to the living room half an hour later, he tossed the front page into her lap.

"Here's some news that may interest you, Kay. Read the story in column four. It's about a friend of mine."

"You mean the story about the Sewell case?" she asked.

"Yes, that's it. I knew Norman Sewell fairly well. I knew a cousin of his even better. He went to my college."

Kay read the newspaper story. Norman Sewell, the son of Howard Sewell, a noted banker, was missing. Detectives had been unable to trace the young man, and a reward of five thousand dollars was offered for information regarding his whereabouts.

"Five thousand dollars!" Kay exclaimed. "That's a nice reward. Do you think he was kidnapped?"

"You haven't read the last paragraph."

Kay scanned the paper again. "It says that a girl named Shirley Hoffman is also missing."

"And what does that suggest to your active mind?"

"That they might have eloped."

"That's just what I decided when I saw the story. If I remember correctly, Sewell always was a romantic."

"Why don't you suggest the idea and claim the reward?" Kay said, laughing.

"I'll suggest it for free, but I think Norman's father thought of it already. Finding the couple is another matter. Norman's probably afraid his father is angry and will keep out of sight with his bride until he figures Mr. Sewell has cooled off."

"Something else might have happened to Norman," Kay said. "You're only guessing that he eloped. It seems to me his disappearance would be the first thing a good detective would investigate."

"True," Bill acknowledged, frowning. "If a five-thousand-dollar reward has been offered it stands to reason the case isn't as simple as it appears. I hope nothing serious has happened to Norman Sewell."

"I'd love to earn that reward," Kay declared as she

read the newspaper story a second time. "I could use some extra money."

There was a knock at the door and Mrs. Tracey went to answer it. She didn't know the woman who stood on the porch, but Kay and the twins recognized Mrs. Vernon at once.

"Do you have a telephone?" the policewoman asked before anyone could speak.

"No, we don't," Mrs. Tracey replied regretfully. "When we came we didn't know how long we'd be here so we didn't have a phone installed."

"My cottage has been robbed," Mrs. Vernon said tersely. "This afternoon, while my sister and I were away, someone broke a window and took about sixty dollars' worth of things. I want to phone the police."

"Another robbery!" Mrs. Tracey gasped.

"I'll drive you to the police station, Mrs. Vernon," Kay offered.

"I'd be very grateful. I want to report the theft immediately. From all I have heard, the police in this district are very slack."

"They haven't been too clever up till now," Bill admitted.

Bill went with Kay and Mrs. Vernon. During the ride to town the policewoman said she was sure the various robberies in the neighborhood were the work of one person. Kay's thoughts leaped at once to Ben Wheeler, but she did not say anything. Bill also said nothing.

"If the twins will help me, I'll follow Ben tomorrow," Kay decided. "I don't want to get him in trouble, but if he's guilty I can't go on protecting him."

At the police station Jane Vernon made a complete report to Chief Benson. She was treated very respectfully, and Sergeant Kelley, assigned to the other robbery cases, was detailed to go at once to the Vernon cottage. Kay was amused to see that the policewoman was not very impressed with the sergeant.

At the cottage Kelley failed to find any worthwhile clues. Mrs. Vernon was obviously annoyed, but she kept her thoughts to herself and said, "I may work on this myself. I reported it as a matter of routine, but I expect to find the thief if no one else shows any interest in tracking him down."

"Don't worry, we'll get the culprit," Sergeant Kelley assured her. "We've been digging at the case for the past week. I expect to make an arrest within forty-eight hours." —

"I hope you don't try to arrest poor Mr. Swope," Kay said. "I'm sure he's innocent."

Sergeant Kelley left the cottage in a bad mood. After talking over the case with Mrs. Vernon, Bill and Kay drove back to their own cottage.

"I'm going to drive to Brantwood tomorrow," Bill remarked as they rode along. "I'd like to talk with Mr. Sewell and see if there's anything I can do to help him find his son. Would you like to go with me?"

"I'm having too interesting a time here," Kay answered. "I'd rather stay."

In the morning the three girls set out to find Ben Wheeler. They hung around the beach for hours hoping to catch a glimpse of him.

"I wouldn't be surprised if he were avoiding me on purpose," Kay told her friends. "Probably he's afraid he said too much."

"We're only wasting our time waiting for him," Wendy complained. "He may not show at all."

"We might check out another angle," Kay suggested after a moment. "Let's see if anyone around here has a boat called the *Rover*."

Anything which involved action appealed to Wendy and Betty, who were all for the change in plans.

The three made their way to the nearby river. Walking along the wharves they looked at the various boats. When the *Rover* did not turn up, Kay asked several boatmen who were loitering by a storage shed. No one had heard of the boat.

"It's just what I suspected," Kay declared. "Ben was probably lying. I doubt he ever went near a boat."

"The boat might have sailed somewhere else," commented Betty, "but it's not very likely."

They walked slowly on down the wharf. Soon they approached a boat which was being repainted. Wendy and Betty paid little attention to it after noticing that it was named *Florence Ann,* and were startled when Kay stopped short and cried in an excited undertone:

"We've found our boat!"

"Not the *Rover,*" Wendy replied, glancing along the river front in bewilderment. "I've looked at every name——"

"The visible ones, maybe," Kay answered. "But look closely at the *Florence Ann.* Just beneath the name you can see another, just visible through the white paint."

"Kay's right!" Betty exclaimed gleefully. "I can make out the old name. It's the *Rover!*"

XI

A Black Jet Button

As they stood staring at the boat, Kay saw two men approaching. They wore overalls and carried paint buckets, and she immediately guessed that they were overhauling the *Rover*.

"Let's get out of sight and watch them," she suggested in a low voice.

Before they were seen by the men, Kay and the twins slipped into the doorway of a warehouse. The men did not glance in their direction but jumped onto the *Rover* and began to work.

"One of those men looks a little like the heavy-set man we saw peering through the Crowley sisters' window," Kay whispered to Wendy and Betty. "Don't you think so?"

"I really couldn't tell," Wendy replied doubtfully.

"His build is the same," Betty acknowledged. "But a lot of men are heavyset."

The girls were close enough to the boat to hear the men talking. However, the painters had very little to say. They discussed a number of things, none of which were of any interest to Kay. The girls did get the impression that the boat was owned by a man who intended to offer it for sale after it had been fixed up.

"We might learn more by questioning them," Wendy suggested finally.

They came out of their hiding place, circled the

warehouse, and leisurely walked up to the *Rover*. There they stopped, pretending to watch the work. The men paid no attention to them until Kay said something. The reply was brief, but refusing to be put off, she next asked the workers if they knew who owned the boat.

"We own it," one of the men responded gruffly. "Now run along, sister, and don't bother us. We're busy."

The girls had no choice but to leave. From the conversation they had heard a few minutes before, they were sure that the painter had not told them the truth.

"Probably the owner told them not to reveal anything," Kay said to her companions. "We'll go away for now, but we can come back later and do some more investigating."

On their way back to the Tracey cottage, the girls met Jane Vernon. She stopped to speak to them, and they asked if anything new had developed in the robbery case.

"Not a thing," Mrs. Vernon answered in disgust. "The local police aren't very efficient, in my opinion. But I shouldn't criticize them. I haven't been able to find any clues myself."

"I bet you've solved lots of mysteries," Kay said encouragingly, hoping that Mrs. Vernon would tell about some of them.

"I've helped with several exciting cases. But I've been told you're a detective yourself, Miss Tracey."

"I'm not a professional detective like you, Mrs. Vernon. I've been lucky in solving a few mysteries. That's all."

"She's too modest!" Betty said. "Kay doesn't need training—she has a natural instinct."

"Have you been reading about the Sewell case?" Mrs. Vernon asked abruptly.

"Oh, yes," Kay answered quickly. "Has he been found?"

"Not yet, and the police tell me no new clues have turned up. The reward offered is substantial—I'd like to earn it."

"So would I!" Betty murmured. "Are you working on the case, Mrs. Vernon?"

"I feel tempted to. I came here for a vacation, but this case offers a wonderful opportunity. Aside from the reward, the person who finds Sewell will get a lot of publicity. That might win me a promotion."

"I hope you're successful," Kay declared. "My cousin, Bill, knows Norman Sewell. He's very worried about his disappearance."

"Your cousin knows the family?" the policewoman inquired eagerly. "I'd like to talk to him about the case—he might be able to give me a valuable clue."

"He's in Brantwood today, but I'm sure he'll be glad to help you all he can when he returns."

The girls fell into step with Mrs. Vernon, walking leisurely toward her cottage.

"Won't you come in?" she invited them as they reached the porch. "I have photographs of Norman Sewell and Shirley Hoffman which you might like to see."

Kay and the twins eagerly accepted. They were introduced to Mrs. Vernon's sister Vanessa, a shy, pretty girl in her early twenties. While they chatted with her Jane Vernon looked for the photographs.

"Where did you get the pictures?" Kay asked as Mrs. Vernon placed them in her hand.

"From the local police. As soon as Norman Sewell disappeared, duplicate photographs were sent to nearly every police station in this part of the country."

Kay studied the pictures carefully, making mental

notes. She thought that if she ever saw Norman Sewell or the Hoffman girl she would instantly recognize them.

"These pictures are the best that they could get," Mrs. Vernon explained, "but they were taken two or three years ago."

The girls talked with the policewoman for nearly half an hour, then walked on toward their own cottage. They saw a large group of people gathered on the sand, having a picnic. Kay and the twins had been invited, but had forgotten all about it. They would have gone on without stopping if one of the young women hadn't recognized them.

"Come and have a sandwich!" she called. "We have lots of good things left."

The girls couldn't refuse the invitation. They were handed sandwiches and introduced to most of the people. Betty noticed that one girl who didn't seem to want to meet them separated herself from the group and disappeared down the beach.

"Did you see that woman?" Betty whispered to Kay.

"Not really. Why?"

"She looked a little like Shirley Hoffman. Her hair was the same color."

"A lot of people have blond hair, Betty."

"But I thought her features were similar too. And she sneaked off so quickly."

"I thought she just walked off. She was probably tired of the party."

Betty was a little annoyed because Kay didn't think her observation was important. "I'm sure I'm right," she told herself. "I'll talk to Mrs. Vernon about it as soon as I can."

The party soon broke up and the cottagers separated to return to their homes. Kay and the twins walked along with several people who were going in their direction. Mr. and Mrs. Jacobs, who owned a house not far from the one rented by the Traceys, unlocked their door, then shouted in surprise.

"Someone broke in while we were away!" Mrs. Jacobs cried. "The place is a wreck!"

Kay and the twins ran to the doorway, and with just a glance could see that the robbers had searched everything. Small objects of value had been taken as well as the large sum of money that had been hidden under a mattress. While the girls were examining the house and trying to calm Mrs. Jacobs, they heard a scream from farther down the beach.

"Robbers! Robbers! Call the police!" someone shrieked. "Our house has been robbed!"

"It looks like the thief knew about the picnic and hit the empty cottages," Kay observed.

She was right. In all, four cottages had been broken into. Kay and the twins went with the victims to the police station. There they made a detailed report of their losses.

"We're doing all we can to catch the thief," the harassed Chief Benson assured the angry house owners. "I've assigned a man to patrol the district. But this is a very clever thief and it will take time to catch him."

"It seems to me you've had plenty of time," one man said furiously. "Get busy or we'll call in private detectives."

Kay was worried as she left the police station. She knew that the demands of the cottage owners would force the authorities to take drastic action. She was afraid that they might arrest Henry Swope, just to appease the cottagers.

When they reached the Tracey cottage, Wendy started sewing while Kay did some ironing. They didn't notice Betty quietly slip out of the house. She had made up her mind to tell Mrs. Vernon about the young woman she had seen at the picnic. Soon Kay finished her ironing and put away the board.

"I wonder where Betty is?" she asked Wendy.

"Oh, she probably went out on the beach," Wendy answered without looking up.

Kay stepped to the door but couldn't see her friend. Slipping on a sweater, she strolled along the beach, enjoying the fresh breeze. With no particular destination in mind she turned in the direction of the Crowley home.

"I wish I could find where the sisters buried their treasure," Kay thought. "The wind has swept away every trace of their footsteps."

She walked on for a short distance. Suddenly she halted, staring at a small object lying in the sand at her feet. It was a black jet button. Kay reached down and picked it up.

"This button matches the one I found at the Crowley house!" she thought excitedly. "Maud or Henrietta Crowley must have lost it from a dress! Maybe I'm near the buried treasure!"

XII

In the Sand Dunes

Kay poked about in the sand for several minutes but could find no more signs that the Crowley sisters had passed that way. Pocketing the jet button, she marked the spot with a forked stick. Then she walked back to the cottage, determined to return later and do a little digging.

During Kay's absence Betty had come back from talking with Mrs. Vernon. When they heard about Kay's discovery, the twins were eager to start searching for whatever the Crowleys had buried.

"What do you think the sisters could have hidden in the dunes?" Betty wondered as the girls armed themselves with shovels and went back to the site which Kay had marked.

"They were so poor, it doesn't seem likely anything very valuable could have been buried there," said Wendy. "But I'll go nuts if we go back to Brantwood without finding out."

"We have a real clue now," Kay said with satisfaction. "I'm sure the jet button came from either Maud's or Henrietta's dress."

The girls took turns at digging but the results were discouraging. They worked for over an hour and found nothing.

"This looks hopeless," Wendy complained, throwing down her shovel. "My hands are blistered already."

"Let's walk on a few steps and try again," Kay persisted. "I'll do the digging."

As they moved, Betty scuffed her shoe through the loose sand, turning up what appeared to be a piece of soiled cloth. She kicked it aside. With a cry, Kay reached down and snatched up the article.

"An old glove!" she exclaimed. "It looks like a mate to the one we found at the Crowley home."

"You're right!" Betty agreed.

"Now we must be getting somewhere," Wendy said, her enthusiasm returning.

The girls dug furiously, but they found nothing else. They were wearily turning up sand when Ben Wheeler slouched into view. He paused to stare at the girls. They couldn't help feeling sorry for him. He looked thin and unhappy.

"That looks like hard work," he observed. "Did you lose something?"

"It's lost, all right," Kay said quickly before the twins could give an explanation which might make him suspicious. "I doubt we'll ever find it now. By the way, Ben, I've been meaning to ask you about that boat you mentioned the other day—the *Rover*——"

A frightened expression came over his face.

"I'm in a hurry now," he interrupted hastily. "I've got to meet a friend."

He walked quickly toward the woods, never imagining that Kay had mentioned the subject on purpose to get him to leave.

"Shall we go on digging?" Wendy asked wearily. "I feel as if I've had almost enough for one day."

"We may as well stop and try again tomorrow," Kay agreed reluctantly.

They slung the shovels over their shoulders and would have carried them back to the cottage, if Betty hadn't been struck by a bright idea.

"Why carry these heavy things all the way home? The Crowley cottage is nearby. Let's leave the shovels there and we can get them in the morning."

In a few minutes the three came in view of the little house amid the pines. Kay, who was slightly ahead of the twins, suddenly stopped.

"Isn't that Ben?" she asked.

Wendy and Betty, peering through the screen of trees, saw him standing on the porch of the Crowley house. He was looking into the window.

"It's Ben all right," Wendy agreed. "What's he up to now?"

"Let's find out," Betty suggested.

The girls walked toward the cottage. Ben was unaware of them, but while they were still some distance away he left the window and went into the woods.

Kay and the twins put their tools in the empty shed. Then they stepped onto the porch and peered through the living room window.

"No wonder Ben was interested!" Wendy exclaimed. "The Crowley furniture is back in the house!"

"It isn't their furniture," corrected Betty.

"No. See all those canvasses and boxes of paint," Kay pointed out. "They never had anything like that. The furniture is cheap too."

"Yes, it is," Wendy acknowledged. "I couldn't see very clearly at first."

As the girls stood with their faces pressed against the windowpane, a man wearing wrinkled blue jeans and tennis shoes came quietly up behind them.

"The furniture may be cheap," he said in a slightly sneering tone, "but I happen to like it."

The girls whirled about, embarrassed.

"Get out!" the man said angrily. "I don't like people prying around my place."

"Your place—" Kay stammered, beginning to understand. "We didn't mean to pry; we thought the house was vacant."

"Well, I guess you haven't done any harm. I wouldn't have spoken so sharply, but once before someone broke into my studio and stole one of my best paintings."

"Are you an artist?" Betty asked, awestruck.

"I call myself one. I don't know what other people think of the work of Burnham Quay."

"I guess you rented the place from Mr. Wake?" Kay ventured.

"Yes, I did, but I wouldn't have taken the house if he hadn't promised me I'd be secluded here. Visitors! Why can't they leave me alone?"

"I'm sure they will when they know how you feel!" Wendy snapped, as the three started away.

"Wait a minute," Mr. Quay said more mildly. "I didn't mean to be such a pill, but you've no idea how much hassle I've had from people. For years I've dreamed of painting my greatest picture, beautiful ocean, sand dunes, and lovely cottages. Here I have the perfect setting, but I need solitude to do my best work."

"We understand," Kay replied quietly, while Betty and Wendy nodded. "You won't be bothered after we leave, I think. Few people ever come here."

"I'm glad to hear that," Burnham said in relief. "And I wouldn't mind a visit from you girls now and then as long as you don't talk to me while I'm painting."

Kay and the twins remained silent. They had no intention of intruding again. Betty went to the shed and got the shovels they had left a few minutes before.

"Just some of our property," Kay explained as she noticed Mr. Quay's surprised look. "We thought we could use the shed while it was empty."

"You're welcome to keep your things there," said the artist. "I'll never use it."

"Thank you, but we'll take the shovels home with us," Kay said firmly. She turned to follow Betty and Wendy. "Oh, by the way, I suppose I should warn you."

"Warn me about what?"

"A number of cottages have been robbed here recently. If you value your paintings you'd better keep them under lock and key."

"Thanks for the tip," Mr. Quay replied. By this time his voice had lost all its coldness. "I'll take good care of my canvasses."

Early the next morning Kay and the twins packed a large lunch and set out with their shovels, determined to make a final search for the Crowley buried treasure. As they got near the site where the glove and the jet button had been found, they were upset to find that the area already was occupied. Burnham Quay had set up his easel on the same dune which they had intended to excavate, and was absorbed in sketching.

"Now what are we to do?" Wendy asked her companions gloomily. "It looks as if the temperamental artist is going to be there for the rest of the day. I couldn't ask him to move."

XIII

A Close Call

The girls stood some distance away, watching Burnham Quay at his work. The man didn't glance in their direction once, he was so absorbed in his sketch of the sand dunes.

"Do you think he'll stay there very long?" Betty asked. "I don't see why he had to choose this particular spot."

The girls approached quietly, standing behind the artist for several minutes before he noticed them.

"Well?" he inquired, finally glancing up.

"We—we don't want to interrupt you," Kay stammered. "We just wondered if you're going to be here long?"

"Very likely. Several days, at least. Now run on and don't bother me. The light is just right and I have to work quickly to get this effect."

The girls left. They stopped several yards away where they held a brief discussion.

"A few days!" Wendy exclaimed. "Just our luck! Why didn't we get here first?"

"Because you were too lazy to get out of bed this morning," Betty told her bluntly.

"I don't know what to do now," Kay admitted with a frown. "Mr. Quay's painting is more important, I guess, than our digging project. Still it's a pain to have to wait."

Burnham Quay, glancing up now and then from his sketch, could hear the girls talking in low voices. He saw the shovels, and guessed that they had a special reason for wanting him to leave the site.

"I wonder what they're up to anyway?" he thought. "Oh, well, I got here first and I'm staying."

He went back to work and forgot the girls. They soon went away and did not return until the next morning. The artist was already there. Presenting themselves once more, they asked how the work was coming.

"I made six rough sketches yesterday," he replied, pointing to several small canvasses, each one portraying the scene from a different angle and with various effects of light and shadow.

"They're beautiful," said Wendy.

"Beautiful! Is that the best you can say for them?"

Wendy thought that she was paying the artist a compliment.

"This picture has more than beauty," Kay told him, picking up the smallest canvas. "One feels almost as if the sand dunes were conveying a message——"

"Ah!" Mr. Quay interrupted, his face brightening, "then I caught what I tried to—the desolation of the windswept shore, the poverty of those who follow the sea for their living. I'll paint my masterpiece from this sketch!"

With new enthusiasm he picked up a brush and began to mix paint, completely forgetting the girls. Soon they wandered away and did not return that day.

The following afternoon Mr. Quay watched in vain for them to reappear on the beach. His work was progressing well, and as he sat on a sand dune and looked at the canvas with deep pride he hoped that Kay and the twins would come to admire it. Finally, as the sun sank lower, he carefully laid aside his brushes.

"I will succeed," he told himself triumphantly. "This is the best picture I have ever painted."

The artist got up and stretched his cramped legs. He was tired.

"I think I'll take a swim," he decided. "It'll do me good."

Mr. Quay went back to the Crowley cottage for his bathing suit. Before racing down to the water he paused once more by his easel to admire the painting.

The artist couldn't swim very well, but he enjoyed wading in the shallow water. Soon he went a short way down the beach beyond the point and flung himself in the warm sand. He closed his eyes and slept for half an hour.

"I shouldn't have left my painting all this time," he thought as he awakened and jumped up.

He hurried back to his easel. Horrified, he stared at the painting. In jagged, uneven letters some vandal had painted across the face of the canvas the two words:

"Beat it!"

"My painting!" Mr. Quay cried in rage. "If only I could lay hands on the creep who did it——"

No one was within sight and the footprints which led to and from the easel might have been his own. Mr. Quay could not be sure.

"It was those girls who did it," he told himself. "For days they've been wanting me to leave this place."

Mr. Quay's face grew grim. He would find them and turn them over to the police!

"But nothing will undo what they've done," he thought miserably.

After a while the artist's rage melted somewhat and he began to study his work. The paint was not entirely dry. If he was very careful he might be able to cover up the letters which had been daubed across the picture. At least it was worth trying.

Seizing his brushes, he devoted himself to the canvas. After an hour's work he had succeeded in obliterating the message, but the painting didn't satisfy him the way it had before. Now he thought the colors were too vivid, but the painting was still good—far better than anything he had ever done before.

Gathering up his materials, he carried the painting back to the Crowley cottage. Then he went looking for Kay and the twins, convinced that they were the vandals.

"They're probably hiding somewhere," he told himself. "But I'll find them."

Early that morning the three girls had driven with Mrs. Tracey twenty miles up the coast to see a flower show. Unaware of what was waiting for them when they returned, Kay and the twins talked cheerfully about Burnham Quay. Seeing an unusually beautiful lily at the show, they decided it would be a good subject for a still life.

"The color is incredible," Kay said enthusiastically. "I'd like to buy it for Mr. Quay." The price was rather high, because the flower belonged to an uncommon variety, but she bought it anyway.

Late in the afternoon Mrs. Tracey and the girls were ready to start back to their cottage. Kay had driven over to the flower show, so her mother decided to take the wheel for the return journey. They passed through several fishing villages, pausing once to take a photograph of a cluster of sailboats and once to get a shot of men drying their nets.

As they drove through the little town of Franklin, they were horrified to see another car turn a corner and speed directly toward them.

"Look out, Mother!" cried Kay.

Mrs. Tracey was too frightened to act quickly. As she gripped the steering wheel her daughter reached over and gave it a hard jerk to the right. A head-on collision was averted, but the fenders of the two cars locked for an instant, then the Tracey car went over into a ditch.

Kay and her mother were thrown violently forward, their heads striking the shatterproof windshield. Wendy and Betty landed in a heap on the floor.

"Mother, are you hurt?" Kay gasped, recovering from the shock of the impact. Her own cheek had been scratched and her arm severely wrenched, but she wasn't seriously injured.

"I—I guess I'm all right," Mrs. Tracey answered shakily. "Wendy and Betty——"

"Present," called a muffled voice from behind. It was Betty's voice.

"I think my leg is broken," Wendy moaned.

Thoroughly alarmed, the others hastened to lift her out of the car, but she was able to stand. Her leg had only been twisted.

"We might have been killed," Mrs. Tracey murmured. "The car that struck us must have been going at least seventy miles an hour."

"It probably went right on, too!" Betty said angrily. "A hit-and-run driver!"

However, she was wrong. The car had stopped around the bend. Several men in uniform came running back toward the Tracey automobile.

"Policemen!" Wendy exclaimed.

Both Betty and Kay required first aid treatment for their bruises and scratches. Although Mrs. Tracey had received no injuries, she was suffering from shock. The police officers helped her to a nearby house and there dressed the girls' wounds.

Mrs. Tracey did not feel friendly toward the policemen, pointing out that they might have killed everyone in her car.

"Only the quick thinking of my daughter saved us," she declared severely. "You rounded the corner at a terrible speed, and I didn't even hear your police siren."

"We didn't use it," one of the men admitted. "We were pursuing a couple of thieves who've been active in this district. That accident was bad luck for us as well as for you. We lost the chase."

"I didn't pass a speeding car before we encountered you," Mrs. Tracey said.

"We were chasing an old car with a house trailer attached," the officer explained. "It probably turned down a side street of the village and is miles from here now."

Kay asked for a more detailed description of the trailer.

"Several days ago I saw an old car with a trailer parked on the main street of our village," she said. "Maybe it was the same one."

"That's not unlikely," the police officer agreed. "The trailer has been reported in various towns around here. Unfortunately, it keeps disappearing. Today is the first time we were able to sight it."

"I'm sorry you didn't catch the thieves," Mrs. Tracey said, "but the fact remains that you should have sounded a warning."

"I'll see that your car is repaired free of charge," the officer promised. "Not much damage was done."

The Tracey automobile was pulled from the ditch. The car seemed to run as well as ever. Kay was chosen to drive back to the cottage. After their experience neither Mrs. Tracey nor the twins wanted to drive.

"I can't help wondering if there's any connection between our robbery cases and the thieves the police were pursuing today," Kay said as they drove along.

"What makes you think there might be?" Wendy questioned her friend.

• 92 •

"Only because of the trailer. I think that may be an important clue."

"You might tell Chief Benson," Betty suggested with a smile.

Kay nodded soberly. "I think I will when we get home," she said. "And if he isn't interested I may start looking myself. I have a hunch that the trailer may turn up near our own village."

XIV

An Artist's Anger

As Mrs. Tracey and the girls drove up to their cottage, they saw a stout woman walking away from the porch.

"That's Mrs. Vernon!" Kay exclaimed.

Switching off the motor, she called to the visitor, who turned around and came back toward the car. The policewoman stared first at the battered fender, then at Kay's bandaged face.

"You've been in an accident," she exclaimed.

"Yes, we all have," Kay answered. "Come in and we'll tell you about it. I have other news for you, too."

"I can only stay for a few minutes but I do want to hear about everything."

After giving an account of the accident Kay told her about the mysterious couple and the trailer which the police had chased.

"Have you told this to Chief Benson?" Mrs. Vernon asked.

"Not yet."

"I'd go to him at once if I were you."

"You think it's an important clue?"

"I certainly do. I never thought of it before, but a trailer should make a good hiding place for stolen property."

"Yes, it ought to. And whenever the police got suspicious it would be easy for the thieves to move to a new location."

"Let's go to Headquarters right now," Mrs. Vernon suggested. "If you're right about having seen the trailer parked in the village, it's possible the thieves may hang around one of the local camping sites."

Kay was pleased by Mrs. Vernon's interest, and the two set off for the village. Chief Benson received them politely, but a slight smile flickered over his face at mention of the trailer.

"I am glad you brought this to my attention," he said, "but I'm afraid I can't do much with it. You can't expect me to arrest a man just because he happens to own an old car and a trailer."

"The police at Franklin consider the occupants to be suspects," Kay assured him.

"In that case I'll hear from them by tomorrow."

"Tomorrow may be too late," Mrs. Vernon protested.

By this time it was perfectly clear to Kay and the policewoman that Chief Benson had no intention of combing the local camps for the thieves.

"Don't be so impatient," he said gruffly. "Give us time and we'll make an arrest."

"Henry Swope?" Kay asked, trying to control her irritation.

"Yes, I'm having him followed. Sooner or later he'll betray himself. Swope is the thief, I'm sure of that. I'll be glad to see the dirty rat in jail."

Chief Benson spoke so strongly, that Kay looked up at him speculatively. A flicker of hatred in the man's eyes revealed that his feeling toward Henry Swope was not impersonal.

"Guilty or not guilty, Benson intends to get that poor guy into jail," Kay thought. "There is more behind this than there seems to be. I think I'll try to find out if there's been a feud between them."

Kay and Jane Vernon left the police station, thoroughly disgusted with the chief. The next day Kay and her friends questioned several villagers to see if Chief Benson might have any reason for disliking Henry Swope personally.

"Well, now," said one old fisherman with a chuckle, "maybe he can't bear the sight of young Swope on account of his Dad. Ezra Swope made a monkey out of Benson, and the Chief never forgot it."

"Did Ezra Swope live here too?" Kay said quickly.

"The Swopes were one of the earliest families," the fisherman told her, puffing at a pipe. "In those days they had money and lived high. Ezra owned the land where the St. Alton Hotel stands now."

The girls nodded. They had admired the imposing white buildings.

"Ezra made plenty of money when he sold his land," the fisherman continued, "but since then it's all been lost. After Ezra died, his son Henry moved away. Folks tell me he came back a few months ago with his family, and they've been having a hard time to make ends meet."

"Yes, that's true," said Kay. "But you were saying something about a feud which existed between Chief Benson and the Swopes."

"It all started before Swope sold his land. He was an old-timer here and considered himself a pretty good historian. Benson hadn't been taken into the police force yet. He was trying to get started as a writer."

"A writer!" Kay exclaimed.

"It was a laugh for everyone all right, but Benson took himself seriously in those days. Swope and Benson both wrote a history of the county, only Swope got his together first. They were good-natured rivals at the start, but after a while they began to fly at each other's throats. Both wanted the honor of having the only published history."

"That sounds pretty silly," commented Betty.

"Sure it was silly, Miss. Then one day Benson's manuscript disappeared."

"Stolen?" asked Kay.

"Well, that's what Benson thought. He openly accused Swope of having taken it, but Ezra just laughed in his face. Then Ezra's history was accepted for publication and that made Benson sore as a hornet."

"Did the book ever appear in print?" Wendy asked.

"Yes, and that's how Ezra got most of his money. He bought land with it, and in only a few months had sold out at a big profit to the hotel people."

"What happened to the fortune?" Kay asked curiously.

"Ezra managed to spend most of it before he died. He left some to a daughter. His son Henry didn't get anything."

"That's too bad," Kay remarked. "He sure needs it now."

She had learned enough to be certain that Chief Benson wanted to send Henry Swope to jail just to get revenge. All these years he had nursed a grudge, waiting for a chance to even up the score. As the girls walked slowly back toward the cottage, Kay told the twins she intended to make a bigger effort to find the real thief.

"I never did believe that Henry Swope had anything to do with the robberies," she declared. "I couldn't understand why the police were trying to pin the crime on him. Now it's all perfectly clear."

"A man in Chief Benson's position has no right to be so prejudiced," Wendy affirmed. "I'm sure he told

Sergeant Kelley and his other officers to try to get any kind of evidence against the man."

"Chief Benson is so concerned with his grudge that he doesn't care whether the real thief is caught or not," Kay said.

The girls had been so absorbed in their conversation that they didn't see Burnham Quay approaching from the opposite direction. Earlier in the day they had taken the lily to his cottage, but finding him out, had left it on his doorstep with a note. Now as Burnham stopped them they assumed that he was going to thank them for the gift.

"Well, I've caught up with you at last," he began wrathfully. "Of all the mean, contemptible tricks——"

"Didn't you like the lily?" Betty interrupted, shocked by his tone. "We thought you would like it."

"Lily? What lily?"

"The one we left on your porch. Kay bought it at the flower show yesterday. She thought it might make an interesting still life."

"I haven't been back to my cottage since I left it early this morning. I don't know anything about a lily. But I do know you girls were the ones who ruined my painting."

Kay and the twins stared at Mr. Quay in astonishment. They had no idea what he was talking about.

"Has something happened to your painting?" Kay asked.

"Don't pretend you don't know."

"But how could we? Wendy, Betty and I were gone all day yesterday. We were at a flower show down the shore. On the way back we had an auto accident." Kay pointed to her bandaged face.

Burnham Quay calmed down a bit, but he wasn't certain that he believed the girls.

"You deny that you painted '*Beat it*' across my picture?"

"Of course we didn't do that!"

"Then tell me why you were always trying to get me to move! When I stayed where I was you ruined my painting!"

"That isn't true," Kay retorted, getting more and more irritated. "I don't know who scribbled on your painting, but we had nothing to do with it."

"You didn't answer my question."

"What question?"

"Tell me why you wanted me to move."

Kay and the twins looked at one another. There was no reason to tell him their secret.

"Our reason doesn't have anything to do with you or your picture," Kay told him. "I don't blame you for being angry about your painting. If you like I'll try to help you find the person who did it."

"That is very kind of you, I'm sure," Burnham said mockingly. "Thank you, I already know who the culprits are."

He turned away without giving the girls an opportunity to reply.

"Boy, is he rude," Betty declared with a shake of her head.

"I wish you hadn't wasted that lily on him," Wendy said to Kay.

"So do I now," said Kay. "He'll probably tear it to shreds when he finds it on his doorstep."

The next morning the girls saw him at his usual spot on the sand dunes. They were careful not to get close enough to speak to him.

"I bet he'll stay there forever," Betty said with a groan. "He knows we want him to move and he'll stay there just to get even."

"He's another Chief Benson," Kay added gloomily.

For lack of anything else to do the girls wandered through one of the tourist parks looking for an old car and a battered trailer. When they returned from that unsuccessful search they found that the mail had been delivered.

There was a letter for the twins from their mother, and they were immediately absorbed-in reading it. Kay picked up an envelope addressed to her. It had been postmarked from a small town in New York and the handwriting was unfamiliar.

She opened the letter, glancing at the names signed on the bottom. Wendy and Betty didn't hear her quiet gasp of astonishment. But a moment later she cried excitedly, "I've gotten a letter from the Crowley sisters!"

"Henrietta and Maud?" asked Betty, looking up. "That's a surprise."

"They are asking for the most incredible favor," Kay revealed, her eyes very bright. "Just listen to this!"

XV

A Strange Request

Kay read the letter to Betty, Wendy and Mrs. Tracey. Although both the Crowley sisters had signed the letter, it was Maud who had written it. The note began by saying that the sisters were at the Thornton Home, near New York City.

"You may be surprised to receive this letter from us and to see the above address. You were probably told that Henrietta and I are staying with relatives in New York. We are very unhappy here, but I won't trouble you with all of that.

"My purpose in writing is to ask you a very great favor. Our departure was hurried, and in our dilemma we did not know what to do with a certain box in our possession. In panic we buried it in the sand dunes not far from our home. Among other things the box contained a message and a signature, and we feel that we must have these papers again.

"Henrietta has not been well, and I doubt either of us will be able to return to dig up our precious box. We thought that considering your great kindnesses in the past, you might be willing to help us recover our treasure. We do not wish to put in writing where the box was buried, but if you are able to come to the Thornton Home for a visit, we will give you instructions."

There was more to the letter. Maud Crowley went

on at some length thanking her friends for previous favors. When Kay had finished it she looked at the twins for their reaction.

"If we ever needed an excuse for digging up that box, we have it now!" Betty cried enthusiastically.

"We sure do," Wendy nodded. "What in the world do you suppose is hidden in the thing?"

Mrs. Tracey hadn't said anything. She was glancing nervously toward the window.

"What's the matter, Mother?" Kay asked, noticing her tenseness.

"I thought I heard a sound. It was as if someone were standing by the window. A stick crackled."

Kay went to the door and looked out. The yard was empty. She had not been quick enough to see a figure hurry behind the house.

"No one's there," she reported, closing the door again.

"Then I must have imagined it. Since the robbery, the slightest sound scares me."

"What are we going to do about the Crowley sisters' request?" asked Wendy, going back to the original subject.

"I wish we could go talk to them," said Kay.

"There's no reason why you can't," Mrs. Tracey replied. "The train trip wouldn't be long or expensive."

"But I don't want to leave you here alone, Mother."

"I've taken care of myself for a long time," Mrs. Tracey smiled. "I'm sure nothing's going to happen to me."

Kay laughed. "I was thinking of the robberies," she said. "I wouldn't want you to be alone at night."

"Bill plans to be back tomorrow, you know, Kay. Unless he changes his plans at the last minute, he'll be here."

"Then let's take the morning train, and go to the

Thornton Home," Kay said enthusiastically. "Those poor old ladies need help."

"Aren't you a little interested in the box too?" Betty inquired mischievously.

"That's understood." Kay laughed. "And since Maud mentioned a signature and a message, I'm even more curious than before."

Not knowing that anyone besides themselves knew the Crowley sisters' secret, the girls made plans to take the ten thirty-five train the next morning. Bill drove in from Brantwood only a few minutes before it was time for them to go to the station. The girls had no chance to talk with him or find out if he had learned anything new about the Sewell case.

After arriving at the station and buying their tickets, they waited out on the platform.

"Isn't that Ben Wheeler?" Wendy asked suddenly, pointing to a boy leaning against the sunny side of the building.

"Yes, it is," Kay declared. "I wonder if he's going somewhere."

They walked over to ask him, but Ben told them he was just trying to kill some time.

"You're not leaving, are you?" he asked Kay anxiously, noticing her suitcase.

"Yes, we are." Kay didn't explain any further. "I'm sorry you didn't go home to the west."

Ben looked away. He seemed to be very moved.

"I can't go," he said. "I'm in it now and I've got to stick it out."

"In what?" Kay asked. "Tell us."

"I can't do that, either," Ben muttered. "You're the only person that was ever decent to me. I'd like to tell you everything, but I just can't."

"I hope you haven't done anything illegal," Kay said, looking at him closely.

"Oh, no, nothing like that!" Ben laughed nervously. He turned away. "Well, I guess I'll be going."

"Good-bye, Ben," Kay said quietly. "If I don't see you again, I hope you think over my advice."

"You're not going away for good, are you?"

"I'm not sure," Kay answered evasively.

"I—I hate to see you go. You're the closest thing I have to a friend."

Kay hadn't realized that Ben thought so much of her. She regretted letting him think she might not return. However, she had hoped that by not revealing anything she might get him to talk.

"I wish I could tell you about something—" Ben began hesitantly.

The girls could see that he was having a battle with himself, trying to decide whether or not to tell his secret. Before he could make up his mind they heard a shrill train whistle.

"Our train!" Betty exclaimed. "Wendy and I have to get our bags from inside the station."

Kay waited, hoping that Ben Wheeler would make some last-minute revelation. The sound of the whistle seemed to have broken the spell. With only a muttered "good-bye" he walked away hurriedly.

"Another moment, and he might have told me everything," Kay thought regretfully. "We'll probably never have another chance like that again."

Wendy and Betty brought their bags from the station. The train thundered in, and the girls found seats toward the middle of a car. As they settled themselves for several hours' ride, they glanced out the window. Kay noticed that they were passing through the western outskirts of Seaside Beach, a section she had never seen before. Houses thinned out rapidly, then the train flashed by a public camping ground.

There were several tents and a few trailers; one in

particular caught Kay's attention. It was a dilapidated, homemade affair, with a name painted across the body of it in big gold letters.

Kay strained her eyes to read the name. She couldn't be certain of it, because the train was traveling very fast by this time, but the word appeared to be *Rover*.

"Hey!" she cried. "Look at that trailer!"

Wendy and Betty turned their heads but they were not quick enough. The train had passed the park.

"We missed it," Betty declared regretfully. "What did you see, Kay?"

"An old trailer which looked like the one the police are searching for. It had a name printed on it. I'm almost sure it said *Rover!*"

"You've forgotten—that's the name of a boat," Wendy said, teasing, "or a dog. I'm afraid——"

"That I have the name *Rover* on my mind." Kay interrupted. "Well, I'll admit I might be wrong. The train was traveling too fast for me to catch more than a glimpse of the trailer. But if the name wasn't *Rover* it was something like it. I'm sure of the last four letters."

While Kay continued to think about what she'd seen, Betty and Wendy promptly forgot it. They were sharing a newspaper and didn't notice that their friend was lost in thought.

After a two-hour ride the girls began to get restless. They were relieved when the porter told them that there would be a ten-minute stop at the town of Atlas.

They left the car with several other passengers and walked up and down the platform. Betty saw a magazine counter inside the station and remembered that she was almost out of things to read.

"I'll be back in a minute," she called suddenly.

"Where are you going, Betty?" her sister asked anxiously.

"Just inside to buy something to read. It will only take me a minute."

"You have about seven minutes," Wendy warned her, glancing at her watch.

Betty disappeared within the station. Kay and Wendy continued their walk. Soon passengers began boarding the train.

"I wish Betty would hurry up," Wendy said nervously, glancing toward the station.

"She's had time enough to buy out the whole magazine stand."

Again Wendy looked at her watch. "She has less than two minutes!"

"We'll have to get her."

Kay and Wendy ran into the depot but Betty was nowhere to be seen. The magazine stand was deserted.

"Where can she have gone?" Wendy cried. "She'll miss the train—and so will we!"

XVI

A Troublesome Cat

"All aboard," called the conductor, waving his hand in signal to the engineer.

Kay and Wendy were in a fix. If they stayed in the station another instant they would miss their train; but they didn't want to leave Betty behind. What had happened to her?

Suddenly Kay saw her some distance away, calmly mailing a letter.

"Betty!" she called frantically to her friend.

The train had started to move. When she heard her name, Betty jumped. She had lost track of the time, and had bought several things in the station.

She shut the mailbox and raced toward Kay and Wendy. The three ran madly across the platform in time to jump aboard the last car. Even then they wouldn't have made it without the help of a young girl in a tweed suit who helped them scramble onto the steps.

"Thank you," gasped Kay. "That was close."

"It sure was," the girl who had helped them replied with an amused smile.

"We must have looked wild racing across the platform," said Wendy.

When they had caught their breaths, they introduced themselves to the young woman in the tweed suit and learned that she was Jessica Webb, a business-woman who traveled frequently.

Kay asked her to sit with them, so Jessica joined the threesome.

"I'm on my way home now," she told her new acquaintances. "Huxley isn't a very large place but I'll be glad to see it again."

"We're going to Huxley, too!" Kay exclaimed.

"Have you ever been there before?"

"No, this is our first visit. Tell me, have you ever heard of a home for old ladies called the Thornton Home?"

"Sure I have. It's in the eastern part of Huxley. Oh, I could tell you a lot of stories about that place!"

"It has a bad reputation?" Kay asked quickly.

"Oh, no, I think it's a fairly good home. But some of the old ladies who stay there are eccentric. I remember one of them in particular. She had a big argument with the authorities because the regulations said she couldn't bring her cats with her."

"The home won the battle, right?" Wendy asked.

"No, the woman somehow got her own way. The last I heard, the cats were still with her."

"We're going to visit two sisters who recently moved into the place," Kay explained. "They're both lovely women."

"I feel sorry for them, going there," Jessica replied. "I'm not saying that most of the women there are weird, but the ones that are stick out."

She told the girls about other strange characters she had met at the Thornton Home. By the time the train pulled into Huxley, Kay was convinced that Henrietta and Maud Crowley never would be happy there.

It was dinner time when the girls arrived. They didn't know of a good restaurant in the town so they were going to try the railroad lunch counter.

"Oh, it's disgusting," Jessica protested. "Come with me to my apartment and I'll cook you a real meal."

The girls didn't want to impose on her, but when she made it clear that she wasn't inviting them just to be polite, but because she wanted to get to know them better, they gladly accepted. After a very good dinner at her apartment, Jessica drove them to the Thornton Home in her car.

"I hope we can stay here for the night," Wendy remarked as the three walked up the cinder path. "Otherwise, we'll have a long walk back to a hotel."

The Thornton Home was a large square building shaded by elms. A few empty benches decorated the lawn.

"It isn't a bad looking place," Betty commented. "But it seems cold and unfriendly."

"All institutions look that way to me," Kay replied as she pressed the doorbell.

A maid appeared and escorted them to an office, where they were greeted by a Mrs. Hackett.

"What can I do for you?" she inquired.

Kay explained that she and her friends had come to see the Crowley sisters.

"Oh, yes, they are expecting you," said the woman. "However, you will find it difficult to talk with Henrietta. She is barely able to whisper."

"Is she very sick?" Kay gasped.

"Oh, no, only a bad cold which settled in her throat."

"And her sister—how is she?"

"Quite well, I believe. Her only trouble seems to be that she can't adjust herself to this place. She misses her old home, but no doubt she'll get over it."

Mrs. Hackett told the maid to take Kay and the twins to the sitting room, where twenty old ladies were having their social hour. The Crowleys were at the far end of the room, somewhat apart from the others. Their faces were sad and they weren't sewing or talking as the women around them were.

Kay and the twins hurried toward them.

"Oh, we knew you would come," Maud said, light coming into her wrinkled face. "It was so kind of you."

"Yes, so kind," Henrietta added in a whisper.

"Don't try to talk," Kay said sympathetically. "Mrs. Hackett told us you have a bad cold."

"Tell me about everything," Maud urged with pathetic eagerness. "The old house is still empty, of course?"

"Well, no, it isn't," Kay admitted. "Mr. Wake rented it to a man named Quay. Didn't he tell you about it?"

"We haven't heard from Mr. Wake since he sent us here."

"We've heard from no one at home," Henrietta added in a whisper. "We feel so isolated and alone."

Kay did not see how anyone could feel isolated or alone at the Thornton Home. The room buzzed with conversation, and the chairs were pushed so close together that you scarcely could walk between them.

"Isn't there some quiet place where we could talk?" Kay asked the two women.

"Not now," Maud said. "We have to go to bed soon."

"We will talk with you in the morning," Henrietta whispered. "Then we'll discuss the matter about which we wrote."

A few minutes later, when the eight-thirty bell marked the end of the social hour, Kay and the twins returned to the office to see if they could make arrangements for the night.

"Certainly," Mrs. Hackett said, "but I have to charge you five dollars apiece."

"That's okay," Kay replied, amazed at the low rate.

However, when they saw their barren rooms, they felt like they were being overcharged.

"If this is a sample of a guest room, the regular rooms must be awful," Betty said. "You couldn't pay me to stay here more than one night."

"I feel even more sorry for the Crowleys than I did before," Kay said sadly as she and the others got ready for bed.

Just as Kay reached up to snap out the light there was a knock on the door.

"It is Maud Crowley. I must talk with you a minute."

Kay quickly opened the door and the old lady came in. She was very excited.

"What is it?" Kay asked. "Is anything wrong?"

"Oh, yes—no, I mean," Maud contradicted herself nervously. "I couldn't talk with you in the parlor. I had to come here. You can't tell anyone why you are here."

"I'd never do that, Miss Crowley."

"Do not mention the subject to a soul in this institution. No one is to be trusted. They are all malicious gossips."

"We'll keep your secret," Kay promised. "Don't worry about it, Miss Crowley. In the morning we'll talk about everything."

The old lady had worn only a thin robe over her nightgown, and now stood shivering from the cold. She didn't seem to know what to do.

"I'll go with you back to your room," Kay offered.

She walked with Maud down the dark, gloomy hall to a tiny room in another wing of the building. Kay didn't stop to look at the room, but helped Maud into bed, then hurried back to her own section of the place. With no light in the corridors she took a wrong turn, and found herself in still another wing.

"I'll probably be wandering around here all night," Kay thought impatiently. "I can't see why they turn out all the hall lights so early. I guess it saves electricity."

She groped her way along the wall toward a faint patch of light far ahead of her. Suddenly she tripped over a cat, and its screech frightened her. As she lost her balance, Kay grabbed wildly for support. Her hand touched wires connected with the house telephone and alarm system.

Immediately bells began ringing loudly throughout the house!

"I must have pulled loose a wire!" Kay thought. "Now I *am* in trouble!"

She could hear cries of alarm throughout the building and the sound of running feet. Nurses and attendants ran to find out what had caused the disturbance. Kay was tempted to slip away in the darkness, but put the thought aside. "No, I'll have to stay and face the music," she told herself. "If I don't, someone else may be blamed for it."

XVII

Revenge

Suddenly lights flashed on in the hallway and Kay found herself facing the watchman.

"Did you ring all those alarms?" he demanded angrily.

Before Kay could answer, Mrs. Hackett and several nurses appeared. All along the corridor doors opened and frightened residents began to call and cry out.

"Why, it is you, Miss Tracey," exclaimed Mrs. Hackett sternly. "I hope you aren't responsible for this."

"I'm really sorry," Kay apologized. "I was feeling my way along the hall when I tripped over a cat. As I fell I must have grabbed some wires and pulled them from the wall."

"You tripped over a cat!" Mrs. Hackett cried, almost triumphantly.

"I am sure it was a cat. I heard it meow."

"Oh, I don't doubt you. It was a cat all right. Ella Whitmore's cat! The animal prowls the halls at night. I was sure of it, but Mrs. Whitmore always claims she keeps the animal locked in her room."

"I might be wrong," Kay said. She didn't want to cause the woman any trouble.

"Oh, no, the accident was caused by the cat," Mrs. Hackett replied with satisfaction. "Tomorrow I want you to testify to this before the Board of Managers."

"It wasn't Mrs. Whitmore's fault," Kay began, but Mrs. Hackett silenced her with a wave of her hand.

"Everyone in this institution hates that cat, Miss Tracey. It has caused nothing but trouble. Because Mrs. Whitmore is nearly eighty-five years old, I overlooked a rule and let her keep it. But she promised she would never let it out of her room."

Kay wished the whole thing hadn't happened, but there was nothing she could do about it. In the morning she was called before the Board and asked to tell the members exactly what happened. She tried to take all the blame, but her attempt failed. The managers were determined to get rid of Ella Whitmore's cat.

When Kay had finished her testimony, the animal's owner was called in. On hearing the decision of the Board she burst into tears. Then, when the Board remained unmoved, she turned angrily on Kay.

"I'll get even with you for this," Mrs. Whitmore cried. "If it hadn't been for you and Maud Crowley I could have kept my cat!"

A nurse led Mrs. Whitmore away, and Kay assumed that the incident was closed. She never thought that the old lady would try to carry out her threat, so it didn't occur to her or the twins to lock their rooms when they went down to the parlor to talk with the Crowley sisters.

Although Henrietta's throat was much better, she still had trouble speaking, and her sister did nearly all the talking.

"I have written out specific directions for finding the box that Henrietta and I buried in the dunes," Maud explained, glancing cautiously around the room to make sure no one was nearby.

Kay took the paper, and a quick glance at it confirmed that the hiding place was near where

Burnham Quay had painted his picture.

"I can't tell you the contents of the box," Maud continued apologetically. "I will merely say that among other things it contains an important message in a certain handwriting, which, if revealed, will change the course of my life and that of my sister."

Kay looked at the two women with curiosity but she didn't ask any questions. One thing was fairly clear, however; since leaving their home the Crowley sisters had been in touch with someone unknown to Kay. They had learned something which made it imperative for them to recover the buried box.

"We'll follow your directions carefully," Kay promised the sisters. "I'm sure we'll be able to find the things for you."

Maud removed a small purse from her dress pocket.

"We want to reimburse you for your train tickets," she told the girl. "How much were——"

"Oh, don't worry about that," Kay interrupted. She knew that the sisters didn't have very much money. "We wanted to come and visit you. You don't owe us anything."

The Crowleys wouldn't budge, however.

"We wrote asking you to come here," Maud said proudly. "We will be offended if you refuse to be repaid."

In the end the girls reluctantly accepted the money, secretly making up their minds that for Christmas they would buy the sisters something very special.

Kay glanced at her watch, to remind Wendy and Betty that their train would be leaving the station in about two hours. The girls said good-bye to the Crowley sisters and went to their rooms.

"We have plenty of time," Betty said. "Our bags are packed, and the ride to the station shouldn't take long if we catch the right bus."

"We'll make it easily," Kay agreed, "but I want to get to the station very early. We have to buy our tickets and you never know what might happen on the way. If we miss our train we can't get another till tomorrow."

Wendy went to the closet where she had left her bag.

"It's not here!" she exclaimed. "Betty, what did you do with my bag?"

"What did *I* do with it! I like that! I was just going to ask you what you did with mine."

"Your bag isn't gone too?"

"It sure is! I left it right here by the bed."

"Kay must have moved all the luggage into her room."

At that moment Kay appeared in the doorway. She had heard her friends.

She announced, "My luggage is gone, too."

"Maybe the porter carried everything out for us," Betty said doubtfully.

"I'm sure he isn't allowed upstairs," Wendy answered. "I think someone has stolen our bags!"

"Then we better tell Mrs. Hackett!"

"No—wait. I think we can handle this ourselves," said Kay as the twins started for the door. "I don't think it's an ordinary theft. Someone may have taken our things just to get back at us."

"The woman with the cat!" Betty cried. "She said she'd get even!"

"I was thinking of Mrs. Whitmore," Kay nodded. "I'll go talk with her."

"It won't do any good," Wendy said gloomily. "She'll deny it and we'll miss our train."

"I've got an idea!" Kay exclaimed, snatching a sheet from one of the beds. "I hope it works."

Without explaining her plan, she went down the hall to Mrs. Whitmore's room. The door was slightly ajar and the woman could be seen sleeping in her bed. Kay knocked six times on the door, spacing the raps evenly.

"Who's there?" she said in a quavering voice.

"Your conscience," Kay answered slowly in a deep sepulchral voice.

Draping herself with the sheet, she slipped into the room. Mrs. Whitmore shrieked and nearly fell out of bed.

"Go away—go away!" she screamed.

"Not until you say you're sorry for your evil doings," Kay replied in a disguised voice. She closed the door behind her.

XVIII

The Disguise

"Why did you harm Miss Tracey? Why did you seek retaliation when it was not her fault that you lost your cat?"

"I didn't hurt her," Mrs. Whitmore murmured apprehensively. "All I did was hide her bag in the basement."

"In what part of the basement?" Kay demanded, almost forgetting to alter her voice.

"In—in the l-luggage room. Please, dear g-ghost——"

Kay didn't wait to hear the old lady's plea for mercy. She ran back to Wendy and Betty and told them what had happened.

They ran to the basement, only to find the room locked. It took ten minutes to locate old Mike, the porter, who was cracking walnuts near the furnace.

"Oh, here you are," cried Kay. "We have a little job for you. Will you unlock the luggage room for us?"

"My keys aren't with me, miss," the elderly man protested lazily. "I can't unlock the luggage room without keys."

"Where are they?" Kay asked impatiently. "We have to get in there right away."

"I'm real sorry, miss," Mike drawled as he tried to pick the kernel from a stubborn nut, "but I've forgotten what I did with those keys."

Kay spotted a chain running from Mike's pocket to a metal clip hooked snugly at the top of his trousers. She took one short step toward the porter and jerked the chain quickly. Out came the keys.

"Is the right key on here?" Kay said sharply. "Come on, now! No more stalling. Open that luggage room door or show us which key to use."

"Now listen!" Mike retorted as he seized the keys and put them back in his pocket. "You aren't my boss. You don't pay me any wages. So don't order me around."

Kay tried a different method, offering the man a dollar. He eyed it with interest, but made up his mind to get back at the girls by being stubborn. Kay offered him two dollars.

This time he produced the keys and quickly unlocked the door. Wendy and Betty found their bags, but Kay's suitcase was nowhere in sight. Finally she saw it stuffed behind a trunk which was too heavy for her to move.

Mike tugged at the heavy trunk until Kay could pull out her bag.

The girls couldn't lose any more time if they hoped to make their train. Grabbing their luggage, they quickly left. They waited twenty minutes at a corner for a bus and were thinking of going back to Thornton to call a taxi, when a bus finally came along. They arrived at the train station only two minutes before the train was due.

"I wonder what else will go wrong," Wendy sighed as the three finally boarded the train. "I'm sure of one thing, and that is I'm keeping my eye on Betty at every stop just to make sure she doesn't decide to buy another magazine!"

The trip back to Seaside Beach was uneventful. At Dover, the station before theirs, Peter Wake boarded the train. Kay recognized the elderly man as he came down the aisle and asked him to join them.

"Do you live in Dover?" Betty asked, when Mr. Wake had seated himself.

"Yes, my home is here," he replied. "I usually drive down to the seashore, but today my car is in the garage. I have a lot of property near the cottage you've rented. It keeps me very busy. So far the Crowley cottage has given me more trouble than any of my other property."

"Isn't the house rented?" Kay asked, wondering if the artist had left in the past two days.

"Oh, yes, a man by the name of Quay is staying there, but I'm sorry I ever let him rent it. I'd rather pay Henrietta and Maud Crowley money out of my own pocket to stay there than deal with such a complainer!"

"What's his problem?"

"Oh, he seems to have a dozen of them. He called me this morning to say that I have to repair a leak in the roof. A few days ago he wanted a new screen for the kitchen window. He keeps telling me that I misrepresented the house to him—that I promised he would have a peaceful, quiet place to paint."

"He hasn't found it that way?" Kay asked.

"Quay claims that someone ruined one of his paintings by marking a warning message across the canvas. He believes that a group of girls did it."

Kay and the twins glanced quickly at one another, then at Mr. Wake. They were relieved to see that apparently he didn't know they were the persons under suspicion.

"It seems that people have been peering in his cottage window too, and he says that at night people dig up the sand dunes where he does his work."

"At night?" asked Kay. "Did Mr. Quay give you a description of the people doing it?"

"No, he didn't. I suspect it's mostly imagination on

his part, but I'm going down there today to try to make peace with him."

"Maybe Mr. Quay really did see someone," Betty declared, before she stopped to think.

"What makes you believe that?" Mr. Wake asked.

"Why, I—he doesn't seem like a man who would imagine things," Betty began to stammer. She knew that Kay didn't want her to mention the buried box.

"Whatever the problem is, I must get it straightened out or I'll lose my tenant," Mr. Wake remarked, looking worried. "Since you young ladies live so close to the Crowley cottage, I'd appreciate it if you'd keep an eye on the spot Mr. Quay mentioned. If you notice anything unusual, please tell me."

"Sure, Mr. Wake," Kay promised. "I have an idea about what may be going on there, and I'll try to find out more."

Before the man could ask her what she knew the train came into the station and the three friends went on their way.

"We'd better start digging right away," Kay told her friends when they were alone. "From what Mr. Wake said, some other person is after the Crowley box, too."

"It looks that way," Wendy admitted. "But who could know about it?"

Kay shook her head. "I haven't the slightest idea. We'll just have to hurry up and make accurate measurements and find the box before someone else does."

"I see trouble ahead," Betty declared with a laugh. "The spot is sure to be near the place where Mr. Quay works."

"Maybe we can make him leave," Kay replied. "He's an unpleasant person even if he is a good artist."

The girls glanced around the station and were

pleased to see that Mrs. Tracey and Bill were there to meet them. After giving a full report of their trip to the Thornton Home, Kay asked her cousin if he had succeeded in locating Norman Sewell.

"I've made absolutely no progress with the case," the young lawyer admitted. "While I was in Brantwood I had a long talk with his father, who is inclined to believe that Norman and the girl eloped and went to another state."

"In that case there isn't much you can do."

"No. The puzzling thing is that young Sewell hasn't gotten in touch with his father. If the marriage did take place, why doesn't he send a telegram at least?"

"He may be afraid of his father."

"Mr. Sewell is ready and willing to forgive. From all that I have heard, Shirley Hoffman is an attractive girl. The Sewells were against the marriage because they didn't think Norman was old enough to get married."

As soon as Kay and the twins had rested a while, they dressed in old clothes and started out for the sand dune site. Burnham Quay wasn't around.

"We've got to hurry," Kay warned her friends as she consulted the paper the Crowley sisters had given her. "Mr. Quay might return any minute."

"Read the instructions out loud," Wendy suggested.

"'From the large pine tree by the main road walk forty paces toward the sea. Then ten paces east along the beach. You should then be in view of the Crag Point Lighthouse. Move six steps to the right and dig.'"

"Well, that should be easy, providing our paces are the right length," Betty declared. "Come on, let's try it."

They stepped off the forty paces to the sand dunes, and after taking the ten steps to the east found themselves within view of the lighthouse.

"So far, so good," Wendy cried triumphantly.

"Now six to the right!" Kay called out, counting out loud.

Suddenly she stopped and began to laugh. The final step had brought her to the very spot where Burnham Quay's deserted easel stood.

XIX

Digging for Treasure

"I don't see anything so very funny, Kay Tracey," Betty declared as she stared at the easel. "This ruins everything."

"You're right," Kay replied seriously. "I don't know why I laughed, unless it was that Mr. Quay has gotten in our way ever since we started to search for the Crowley box. I can't believe he chose this one spot to sit and paint when he had miles of beach to choose from!"

"Let's push the easel in the ocean and start digging," Wendy proposed.

Kay shook her head.

"I feel like doing just that," she said, "but we can't. We have to think of something else."

"I don't care about Mr. Quay—not after what he said to us!" Betty declared with feeling.

"I wasn't just thinking of him," Kay replied. "If he gets angry with us he'll go away. That's what we want, but then the Crowley sisters would be left without a tenant. No, we'd better talk to him."

The girls started for the Crowley cottage. They had gone only a short distance when they met Jane Vernon. Not realizing that Kay and the twins were in a hurry, she stopped to talk about the Sewell case.

"I still have high hopes of winning that reward," she declared cheerfully. "This morning I heard from a source which I can't reveal, that Norman Sewell and Shirley Hoffman are honeymooning in this vicinity."

This especially interested Kay, because Bill believed the young couple had been married in another state.

"I'll keep you posted," Mrs. Vernon promised the girls as she continued on her way. "If I learn anything more I'll let you know."

As they approached the old Crowley cottage a little later, Kay and the twins noticed that the front door was open. They heard voices and assumed that Mr. Quay was talking with Peter Wake. Then to her surprise Kay heard some startling words.

"I don't like this, Smoky. It's dangerous!"

"That sounds like Ben Wheeler's voice," she murmured. "Something's wrong here."

The girls cautiously drew closer. They circled the house, and after hiding themselves in some shrubbery, Kay peered in one of the rear windows.

"We were caught doing this once before," Betty whispered nervously. "Can you see anything?"

Kay didn't reply. She was too busy watching Ben Wheeler and a stout, red-faced man as the pair examined a group of Mr. Quay's oil paintings. No one else seemed to be in the cabin.

Did the men intend to steal the pictures? Kay thought they didn't have a right to be in the cabin, though she couldn't be sure. The one called Smoky appeared to be methodical and confident. He thumbed through the paintings with such calm assurance that she thought maybe Burnham Quay might have sent him there to get one of them. Yet that didn't seem logical either. Something was wrong. As Kay watched, Smoky selected two of the larger paintings and wrapped them in old newspapers.

"Come on, Ben," he ordered. "We ought to be getting away from here."

"Let's follow them!" Kay whispered tensely. "They may be stealing those paintings."

Keeping well behind them, the girls trailed the pair to a nearby tourist camp where Ben Wheeler and his companion entered an old-style homemade trailer. Although it had been repainted, Kay pointed out to her friends some faint lettering which spelled *Rover*.

"It's the same trailer I saw from the train," she said excitedly. "And it may be the one the police are searching for."

"If that's so, I guess Ben Wheeler isn't the fine, upright person you thought he was, Kay," Wendy said.

"I was never sure he was absolutely honest," said Kay. "In fact, I always thought that he was worrying about something he'd done wrong."

Smoky got out of the trailer suddenly, and the girls pretended to be interested in something nearby. The man gave them a suspicious glance, and attaching the trailer to his car, he drove away.

"I wish we had our car here," Kay said in disappointment. "I want to follow him and see where he goes."

"Maybe we should tell Chief Benson," Wendy suggested doubtfully.

"He isn't interested in trailers!" Kay replied. "He won't do anything about it. Let's go back to the cottage and see if anything besides the pictures was taken."

The girls went back, but scarcely had they walked into the house than they were startled to hear a groan from a closet. Kay unlocked the door and pulled it open.

"Mr. Wake!" she cried, as the man half fell into the room. "What happened to you?"

Then she saw that he couldn't speak. A strip of tape had been sealed across his mouth. The man sagged into a chair, nursing a large bump on his forehead. The girls ran to the kitchen for water to soak off the adhesive tape.

"Tell us what happened," Kay urged, when Mr. Wake was able to speak.

"I don't remember very well," he murmured. "When I was struck on the head everything went black."

"Who put you in the closet?" Kay asked.

"A young man and a burly man who called himself Hagerty."

"Then they did come to steal Mr. Quay's paintings!" Betty exclaimed.

"Yes, I was waiting here for Mr. Quay, when they appeared in the doorway. They just walked in. The older one said that Quay had sent him to get several paintings. As he examined them I got suspicious. I asked a few questions and then the trouble started. He hit me over the head and pushed me in the closet. I don't remember anything more."

"Was it the boy who struck you?" Kay asked.

"No. The man. He hit me with a piece of stove wood."

While the girls were looking around the cottage to see if anything besides the two paintings had been stolen, Burnham Quay came up the path. He stopped short in the doorway upon recognizing Kay and the twins.

"You here—again!"

The girls didn't speak, and Mr. Quay's gaze roved to Peter Wake, who still looked dazed and ill.

"I was slugged," Mr. Wake murmured. "Some of your pictures were stolen. I tried my best——"

"My pictures stolen!" the artist cried in rage. "And

you stood here and let the thieves get away? Which paintings were taken?"

Quay began to examine the remaining pictures in a frenzy.

"'June Morn' and my sand dune painting are gone!" he exclaimed furiously. "My best works! Oh, this is the last straw!"

"You should go to the police—" Mr. Wake began, but the artist cut him short.

"I don't need advice from you!" he snapped. "As for the police—in this town they are a bunch of nitwits."

"They do represent the law," Kay observed with a slight smile.

Mr. Quay glared at her, and began throwing things into a suitcase.

"I've had enough of this cottage and this town. I'm moving out. I wouldn't stay here another day if you paid me a hundred dollars."

Mr. Wake didn't look very troubled to hear this. As for Kay and the twins, they could not hide their elation. With Burnham Quay gone they could dig for the Crowley box!

The artist, seeing their expressions, wheeled indignantly on Kay.

"Now that you have forced me to leave I suppose you are happy! Not content with ruining a picture and pestering me whenever I want to paint, you engineer this robbery as the final touch!"

"Mr. Quay!" Peter Wake interrupted. "Accusing these girls of instigating the robbery is utterly ridiculous. I saw the thieves with my own eyes."

"Well, maybe they didn't have anything to do with the theft, but they've caused me enough grief without that. All my trouble started the day I caught them spying into my cabin."

Mr. Quay gradually became aware that no one was

listening to his tirade. All eyes were focused on a point beyond him. In surprise he turned and looked toward the doorway.

There stood Ben Wheeler.

XX

Ben's Confession

Ben Wheeler crossed the room and faced Burnham Quay with flashing eyes.

"It's not true what you say about these girls causing
trouble!" he almost shouted. "They had nothing to do
with the robbery, and they didn't ruin your painting."

"I suppose you can tell me who did?" the artist
demanded sarcastically.

"Yes, I can. That's why I came here. I wouldn't do
this," Ben began, "only you've been good to me,
Kay—the one person who has been decent to me since
my parents died."

"When did that happen?" Kay asked.

"A little over a year ago. My mother and dad were
in a bad auto accident out west. Smoky Rover came
along——"

"Smoky Rover?" Kay cut in, glancing quickly at
her friends.

"His real name is Hagerty. Anyway, I thought he
was a good sort. When my parents were nearly dead, he
offered his blood for transfusions.

"It was a trick, but I didn't know that. My parents
died and then Hagerty told me that I owed him
seventy-five dollars for his blood."

"That's outrageous," Betty murmured.

"I didn't have any money after the funeral
expenses were paid. Hagerty said I could work it out if I

wanted to and since I didn't have a job it looked like a good idea. He said we'd travel around in a trailer and that sounded great to me because I'd never been anywhere."

"You came east?" Kay asked as Ben paused.

"Yes, and it didn't take me long to guess that the trailer had been stolen. Hagerty had repainted it. He went from place to place stealing things and selling them in other states. He liked to hang out near summer communities. That was because the cottages were usually left unlocked when the tenants went down to the beach and other places."

"Did you help him with the robberies?" Mr. Wake asked.

"Sure, I had to. I was expected to bring in a certain amount of loot each week. If I didn't, Smoky beat me up."

"Why didn't you leave him?" Wendy questioned.

"Because I owed him money. I kept thinking I'd get out of debt, but Smoky always claimed the things I stole for him never brought in much. He threatened that if I ever told anyone he'd see that I went to jail along with him."

"What brought you here today?" Kay asked curiously.

"I didn't want you to be blamed for something I did. I've repaid my debt to Smoky a dozen times over, and I've had enough of stealing. I sneaked off a few minutes ago while Smoky was asleep in the trailer."

"You'll go to jail, all right!" Burnham Quay cried furiously, trying to grab Ben by the collar. "First you steal my paintings, then you have the nerve to come here and tell us about it!"

"Don't touch him," Mr. Wake commanded. "Let him finish his story."

"Tell us what you know about Mr. Quay's paintings, Ben," Kay urged.

"Smoky intends to take the paintings to a dealer named Keller at a city up the coast—Bellmar, I think it's called. If you watch that place you might get your pictures back."

"I don't believe a word of it!" Burnham Quay snapped. "But I know one thing—this boy is going to jail! The police will get the truth out of him!"

"Oh, will they?" Ben asked mockingly.

As the artist lunged toward him he deftly side-stepped and ran out the door.

"Come back, Ben! Come back!" Kay shouted, but the boy kept running.

"Well, I hope you're satisfied, Mr. Quay," Peter Wake commented coldly. "If you could have kept your temper we might have learned a great deal more."

"Oh, shut up," the artist snapped. "I'm sick and tired of this whole mess. I'm leaving!"

He stalked into the bedroom and could be heard throwing clothes and shoes into his trunk.

"Oh, I shouldn't have said that," Mr. Wake said nervously to the girls. "I've lost a tenant for the Crowley sisters. It's so late in the season the place will probably stay empty."

"Let him go," Kay said. "We'll help you find another tenant, Mr. Wake."

"Yes, we'll help you," echoed Wendy.

"Right now we've got to go to the police station and report all this," Kay declared. "I'm sorry Ben's involved, but it's so clear that he was used by Smoky Rover, nobody can blame him. Wouldn't it be better for Ben to be arrested and tried and acquitted?"

"Yes, if he's acquitted," Mr. Wake replied.

While Burnham Quay was making arrangements

to have his things moved to a village far down the coast, Kay and the twins hurried to the police station. Chief Benson didn't bother to hide his frown when Kay appeared before him.

"Well, what have you lost this time?" he asked bluntly.

"Nothing," Kay answered. "I have some information which I think will solve the robberies committed around here in the past few weeks."

"Indeed? Well, that's interesting."

Kay ignored the sarcasm and began her story. She could see that Chief Benson was impressed, but he pretended to be only mildly interested.

"The boy very likely made up the entire story," he said when she had finished. "I still feel as I have from the first—that the thief is Henry Swope. Unfortunately I haven't been able to obtain enough evidence for an arrest, but I hope to make one soon."

Kay was at a loss for a moment and wondered how bold she could afford to be. She decided to take a chance.

"You're trying to railroad an innocent man into jail while you let the real thief escape!" she said indignantly. "People around here have lost patience with the way you're handling these robbery cases. And all because you're holding a grudge."

"A grudge?"

"Yes, isn't it true that you believe Henry Swope's father stole your manuscript—your history of the county?"

Chief Benson's face became a cherry red. He looked so angry that Kay thought he intended to deny the charge. However, he answered evenly, "I don't know how you learned that, but it is true. Ezra Swope did steal my manuscript. But that has nothing whatsoever to do with the present case."

Kay thought that it had a great deal to do with Chief Benson's attitude toward his rival's son. Later in the afternoon when she stopped at the Swopes' home to tell them what she'd found out, she told them what she thought of Benson.

"Benson always has had it in for me," Henry Swope declared. "Seems like I ain't strong enough to fight him. If I manage to keep out of jail, it will be because of you."

"You've been so kind to us," Mrs. Swope murmured, tears coming into her eyes. "We'll always remember it."

The visit to the fisherman's shack had taken longer than Kay realized. When she got home she found Wendy and Betty impatiently waiting for her on the porch.

"You've been gone hours," Betty declared. "Wendy and I were hoping that we could dig up the Crowley box."

"Burnham Quay has gone?"

"Yes, we saw a truck take his things away half an hour ago."

Kay checked her watch.

"It's too late to do any digging today," she admitted. "But tomorrow we'll get up early and find it."

XXI

Perilous Waves

The following morning did not dawn bright. Instead, when Kay and the twins got up a little after six o'clock, they were discouraged to find the sky overcast.

"It'll rain in an hour or two," Betty said gloomily. "If this isn't just our luck!"

"We can't afford to put off digging," Kay declared as she dressed quickly and grabbed her raincoat. "Maybe we can find the box before the storm breaks."

The beach was entirely deserted as the girls made their way toward the spot in the sand dunes. They had misjudged the speed of the approaching storm, so that they had scarcely begun work when it started to rain. At first they kept on with the digging, but soon a high wind sent mountainous waves racing across the beach, closer and closer to their site.

"This is a mess!" Betty exclaimed, dropping her shovel. "I'm wet to the skin."

"Those breakers will be washing over this spot if they come much nearer," Wendy observed uneasily. "Look at that big roller—it's twice as large as the others!"

"Run!" Kay yelled. "Do you want to be drenched?"

"We couldn't be much wetter," Wendy laughed as she and her sister raced after Kay beyond reach of the giant wave.

"Oh, my shovel!" Betty suddenly exclaimed.

It was too late to save it. A greedy wave sucked it in and swept back toward the sea. However, the shovel was not carried far, and seeing it, Kay cried out that she would get it.

"No! No!" Betty protested. "It's too dangerous, Kay! Let it go!"

Kay didn't hear her. Before the twins could stop her she had splashed out into the shallow water. As she stooped to pick up the shovel, a wave struck her and flung her on her face.

"Look out!" the twins screamed. "There's another big one coming!"

Kay was struck again before she could get to her feet. Again she was flung violently forward, then the receding wave caught her and she was swept out to sea.

A strong swimmer, Kay still might have saved herself, but for a minute she was hopelessly confused. As she tumbled over and over in the water she had no idea in which direction she was being taken. When she struggled to the surface and recovered her bearings, she was some distance from shore. A few strokes convinced Kay that she could not hope to battle the tide. Her only chance was to go with it.

Kay could see Wendy and Betty waving their arms frantically, but she was too far away to hear their shouted instructions. The next instant, as a huge wave descended upon her, she lost sight of them entirely.

A distance from shore the water wasn't so rough, Kay discovered. While she didn't have enough strength to swim to the beach, she could keep from being swept farther out to sea. The current was gradually carrying her down the coast.

"If I don't panic I'll be all right," Kay told herself. "Sooner or later I'll come to a quiet cove where I can swim ashore."

Her shoes were pulling her down so she kicked

them off. Her other clothes she kept on, knowing that they would protect her a little from the coldness of the water.

Fortunately for Kay, the current swept her toward an amusement park which had been built out into the water. By using all her strength she was able to reach the structure and grasp one of the piles.

"Help! Help!" she began yelling.

When she was beginning to think that no one would ever hear her, she heard an answering shout. A man came running along the pier with a rope in his hand.

"Hang on!" he shouted. "I'll have you out in a minute."

He tossed the line over the edge of the pier, but he was so nervous and excited that he missed Kay. By the time he had hauled up the rope and tried again she was nearly exhausted. She made a big effort and managed to loop the line under her armpits. With the man pulling from above she was able to climb the post to safety.

"Miss Tracey!"

Hearing her name, the dazed and bedraggled Kay looked at her rescuer. For a moment she didn't recognize Henry Swope in his oilskins. The man had been standing near the pier when he noticed a struggling figure in the water. He had dashed into a nearby shed for a rope, and it was his quick thinking that saved her.

"I owe my life to you," Kay gasped.

"Here, let me help you," Mr. Swope urged, half carrying Kay down the pier.

While he was deciding where to take Kay, Wendy and Betty came running toward them. They had never lost sight of their friend. Frantic, they had watched her battle her way down the coast, and from a distance they had seen the rescue.

"Oh, you're alive!" Betty cried as she clasped Kay's icy hand in her own.

"We thought you were going to drown," Wendy murmured. "I've never seen the ocean so violent."

"I couldn't have held out much longer," Kay admitted. "Mr. Swope saved me."

"It was a great rescue," Betty said. "But we can't stand here talking. Kay has to get into some dry clothes."

The girls spotted a building near the pier which had been built for the use of bathers. They led Kay there while Mr. Swope went to get the Tracey car.

"Now sit right here where you'll be protected from the wind," Betty commanded. "Wendy and I will try to get some hot coffee."

When the twins returned ten minutes later with a cup of steaming coffee, Kay signaled them to be quiet.

"Don't make any noise," she warned. "Just look over there in the corner."

She pointed to a huddled figure at the far end of the room.

"Who is it?" Wendy asked in a whisper.

"Ben Wheeler. I noticed him right after you left. He's fast asleep. He seems to be exhausted."

Just at that moment Henry Swope and Mrs. Tracey drove up. Kay gently wakened Ben and persuaded him to go home with her.

"You'll turn me over to the police," he said anxiously.

"No," Kay replied. "I'll give you a decent meal, and then you can decide what you want to do."

Mrs. Tracey hardly noticed Ben Wheeler, she was so upset by her daughter's appearance. She didn't even hear Kay tell her that the boy was going to the cottage with them.

"You must change into dry clothing at once," Mrs.

Tracey urged. "You'll be very lucky if you don't get sick."

While Ben went outside with Mr. Swope, the girls helped Kay change her clothes. She was worried that Ben might run away again, but when they emerged from the building he was still there.

"You can sit up front with Mr. Swope," Kay told Ben as she and the others seated themselves in the rear of the car.

Ben started to get into the car, but with one foot inside, he heard another motor and stopped. A car was coming down the road. The boy stared at it and then exclaimed, "Chief Benson! So this was a trick after all!"

Kay glanced out through the rear window and saw the police chief's car.

"No, it isn't a trick!" she said quickly. "Get back in that building, Ben, and don't make a sound!"

XXII

Hiding a Fugitive

Scarcely had Ben Wheeler slipped inside the building when Chief Benson's car drew up alongside that of the Traceys. The police officer had not seen the boy, but Kay and her friends weren't sure of this.

"I want to talk with you!" the chief said belligerently, indicating Kay.

Before she could speak, his gaze fell on Henry Swope, and instantly the officer's face flushed with anger.

"So you're a friend of the Tracey family, are you?" he demanded sarcastically. "I might have guessed!"

"I haven't done anything wrong," Mr. Swope muttered. "You should stop hounding me all the time."

"Beat it before I snap handcuffs on you!" Chief Benson ordered. "Just looking at your face gives me a pain."

Henry Swope wasn't a man who stood up for his rights. Without a word he left the car and hurried down the beach. He knew he had done nothing wrong, yet sometimes he believed that Benson might be right about his father. Ezra Swope had been a studious, well-educated man, but was he capable of writing a history? Henry Swope often worried that his father might have stolen the Benson manuscript.

"Chief Benson," Mrs. Tracey said coldly after Swope had disappeared down the road, "You didn't have any right to order the man out of our car."

"If you knew him as I do, ma'am, you'd thank me for sending him off," the officer retorted. "Just now I have a little matter to talk over with your daughter."

Kay's pulse was racing. She assumed that the chief had seen Ben Wheeler leave the car.

"Because of you I've wasted six perfectly good hours," the officer said angrily. "I drove down the coast to see that picture dealer whose name you gave me."

"And what did you find out?"

"Absolutely nothing. There is no such person. It was all a hoax as I suspected in the first place. I don't want you bothering the police department any more. If you get another so-called hot tip keep it to yourself!"

"Is that what you came to tell me?" Kay asked, relieved that he hadn't said anything about Ben Wheeler.

"Yes, it is. And say, has anyone been swimming in the ocean?" The chief had noticed a roll of wet clothing lying on the floor of the car. Kay's bedraggled hair was proof enough that she had been in the water. "So *you* broke the rules."

"What rules?" asked Kay.

"There is an ordinance which says that the swimming season officially ended at this beach day before yesterday. I suppose you'll try to tell me you've never heard of it."

"I never have," Kay replied. "But it doesn't matter anyway because I was washed into the ocean by a huge wave."

"That's what *you* say."

"Chief Benson," interrupted Mrs. Tracey, "I resent your attitude. My daughter is telling the truth. She almost drowned just now and Henry Swope rescued her."

"Why didn't you say so in the first place?" the Chief demanded gruffly. "Well, I'll be moving along."

When his car had disappeared down the road, Wendy ran into the building to get Ben Wheeler, who was hiding in a dark corner. The Tracey car then headed home.

"I'm not surprised that you dislike Chief Benson, Kay," Mrs. Tracey remarked. "The man shouldn't hold such a responsible position."

At the cottage Kay took a hot bath and then she and Ben Wheeler had a warm meal. Ben ate as if he were starving, and when asked he admitted that he hadn't eaten for a day.

"I'm out of money too," he said gloomily. "I don't know what to do. Maybe I'll hop a freight and try to get to New York."

"No, don't do that," Mrs. Tracey said instantly. "If you want you can stay here for a day or two until we can work out something for you."

A little later in the bedroom they shared Kay and her mother discussed the situation. They knew it was dangerous for them to hide Ben. Chief Benson would make a lot of trouble if he found out.

"What can we do?" Mrs. Tracey asked earnestly. "I think Ben is at a crossroads in his life. If no one helps him now, he may go back to stealing."

"He sure needs friends now," Kay said.

"We can't keep the boy here indefinitely, though," Mrs. Tracey went on, frowning thoughtfully.

Kay wished that Bill were there to help. He had gone back to Brantwood, and it wasn't likely that he would return to the seaside cottage that summer.

"I think I'll write to Bill tonight," Kay said. "It seems to me that sooner or later Chief Benson will catch up with Ben, and when he does, Ben will need a good lawyer."

Kay wrote a long letter to her cousin in which she pleaded Ben's case. In writing about the theft of

Burnham Quay's paintings, she gave a detailed description of both of them.

"Someday you may run into them," she wrote, "and if you ever do, please tell me right away. At the moment my reputation as a detective is shot."

Kay sent the letter off special delivery. While waiting for an answer, Kay kept busy boosting Ben Wheeler's spirits. He stayed close to the house, helping Mrs. Tracey with cleaning and any other work he might do. She found him to be quiet, serious, and pathetically eager to show his appreciation.

"I can't figure out why Smoky Rover didn't take the paintings to Bellmar," he said more than once. "Maybe he just said that to throw me off the track."

Kay and the twins hadn't forgotten their promise to the Crowley sisters, but the weather was against them. For two days the sea remained high, and between rainstorms they could see the waves lapping at the place where they wanted to dig.

The third day dawned bright and clear. Kay and her friends immediately made plans to resume their search for the hidden box.

"We have only two shovels now instead of three," Wendy reminded the others. "But we should be able to manage. I'll sit in the shade and watch the work!"

"Just for that idea you may run out to the garage and get the shovels," Betty said sweetly. "Don't let Ben see you."

The girls soon were ready to leave, but as they walked down the path Kay saw the mailman coming.

"Oh, wait just a second," she pleaded. "I may get a letter."

The mailman smiled pleasantly as he handed the hoped-for letter to her. Kay glanced at the writing.

"It is from Bill!" she cried.

XXIII

The Stolen Box

Bill Tracey had written at some length, assuring Kay that while he didn't like the idea, he would defend Ben Wheeler just to please her.

"Well, that's a load off my mind," Kay declared after she had read the letter to her friends. "Ben deserves something better than prison."

Armed with shovels, the girls started out again for the sand dunes. Making sure that no one was nearby, they went to work. After an hour Wendy thought that she had found something important when she uncovered a plain gold wedding ring. But it apparently had been lost in the sand years before and had no connection with the Crowley box. A little later Betty found a string of beads. Her excitement died when the jewelry was cleaned off. It was a child's toy necklace.

At twelve o'clock the girls stopped for lunch and a brief rest. They had begun to feel discouraged.

"We might have measured incorrectly," Kay said, frowning. "Maybe we should move our digging operation a little."

The girls paced off the distance again, shortening their steps, and at the new spot they started digging again. As they worked they failed to notice that a man had crept up to a clump of bushes nearby, and was watching them intently. Finally, completely worn out, Kay and the twins decided to call it a day.

"I'm beginning to think someone may have found the box already," Kay remarked gloomily as they trudged toward the cottage. "Either that, or the Crowley sisters made a mistake in giving directions."

"Ben Wheeler is watching us from the window," Betty warned in a low voice. "I think he's noticed our shovels."

"Maybe we should tell him what we're doing," Kay said thoughtfully. "He may know something about the box."

"What makes you say that?" Betty asked quickly.

"Remember someone painted the words *'Beat it'* on Quay's picture? Doesn't that suggest that someone else is interested in that spot?"

"Yes, it does," Wendy answered soberly. "Let's ask Ben."

When they talked with him he pretended at first to know nothing about it. But Kay eventually got him to admit that he and Smoky Rover had guessed that something valuable was hidden in the dunes. The pair had watched Kay and her friends in the area but had never figured out the exact location of the hidden object.

"Then you don't think that Smoky Rover found it?" asked Kay.

"Not while I was with him, he didn't," Ben replied. "But if I know him he'll keep on trying until he does find what he's after."

Ben's remark worried Kay. That evening after Wendy had gone to bed with a headache, Kay persuaded Betty to walk with her to the dunes.

"I'm too tired to do any more digging today," Betty protested, but agreed to go when Kay said that she would do all the work.

The girls had gone a short distance down the beach

when Kay suddenly clutched her companion's arm. She pointed to a shadowy figure directly ahead.

"Why, that man is digging at our spot!" Betty whispered tensely. "He must be after the box! Let's chase him off!"

"No, wait!" Kay whispered. "Let's hide here and watch. If he finds the box we'll claim it."

"Not a bad idea," Betty laughed. "He'll do the hard work and we'll get the box!"

The girls were too far away to recognize the man and they didn't dare come closer for fear he would see them. For ten minutes he worked industriously digging up sand, but at the end of that time he gave an exclamation of disgust. Then, throwing his shovel over his shoulder, he walked away.

"Did you recognize him, Kay?"

"It was so dark I couldn't see him very well, but I thought he looked a little like Smoky Rover."

"So did I," Betty agreed. "I hope he isn't prowling around in this neighborhood again!"

"I wish he'd stay long enough for the police to catch him," Kay replied as the girls turned homeward. "Whoever the man is, he's after our box, and we have to work quickly if we're going to find it before he does."

Before Mrs. Tracey woke up the next morning, Kay, Wendy and Betty made breakfast and ate it quickly. Then they headed for the dunes. They hadn't turned up many shovelsful of sand before Kay found a sheet of paper.

"What is this?" she cried, snatching it up. "A warning note!"

With Betty and Wendy peering over her shoulder she read the note out loud. It had been scribbled in pencil.

"Danger! Do not dig here!" it read.

Kay tore up the paper and tossed it aside.

"Maybe we should give up the idea of finding the box—" Wendy began uneasily, but Betty interrupted her with a laugh.

"Who's afraid of a piece of paper? Pick up your shovel and get back to work. This may be the exact spot where we'll find the box."

An hour passed, but the Crowley box was still not unearthed. Betty lost her enthusiasm.

"Let's go for a swim," she suggested suddenly. "Afterward we can come back here and try again."

"The beaches are closed," Kay reminded her friend with a grin.

"Oh, who cares about Chief Benson!" Betty retorted. "It's hot enough and I want a swim, rules or no rules."

"I think it's a stupid rule," Wendy added. "Even if the lifeguards are gone, the sea is quiet and we'll be perfectly safe."

"You go if you like," Kay said. "I'd rather stay here and dig."

Betty and Wendy went off alone. They returned to the cottage for their suits, and a little later Kay saw them swimming in a secluded cove some distance away.

She kept digging steadily without much hope of success. Then unexpectedly her shovel struck something hard. Her heart leaped. She tossed up another scoop of sand and saw a shiny metal surface. It was a box!

Throwing her shovel aside, she began digging at the sand with her hands. She quickly uncovered the object. The little box was only a foot square, but for its size it was extremely heavy.

Kay started to open it, then the thought occurred to her that she had no right to pry into the Crowley sisters' personal things. She decided to call Wendy and Betty and tell them that she'd found the box. Leaving it on the sand, she ran down the beach, shouting to her friends.

"Wendy! Betty! Come here! I've found it!"

As the twins came out of the water, Kay ran to meet them and told them the news. At the same time a man slipped out from behind the bushes, and snatched up the box. But the girls saw him.

"Drop that!" Kay yelled.

The man only laughed. With the box under his arm he ran across the dunes and disappeared into the woods.

Kay ran after him. The twins, their bathing suits dripping, brought up the rear. They were close enough to see that the thief was Smoky Rover Hagerty.

Kay was fast and she was gaining on him. But just as she began to think that she would overtake him he came to a clearing where his car and trailer were parked. He jumped into the car, and with a wave of his hand, drove off.

XXIV

An Exciting Chase

The three girls ran back to the Tracey cottage for the car. While Betty and Wendy changed out of their bathing suits, Kay talked to Ben Wheeler and got him to say where he thought Smoky Rover might take the trailer.

"Maybe he went down the river," Ben told her. "Smoky has been picking up a little extra cash by carrying supplies to a couple of people over at Brenton Isle. He has a canoe hidden in the bushes and might take the box over to the island."

"Come with us, Ben," Kay urged. "Then we won't make any mistakes finding the place."

With Ben to guide them, the girls soon arrived at the river. Ben searched the bushes for Smoky's canoe, and finding it gone, he was convinced that his theory was correct.

Kay hired a boat from a fisherman and the four rowed across to the island. As they approached, Ben steered to the north side, allowing the craft to glide along the overhanging bushes.

"I don't see Smoky's canoe anywhere," Betty said, gazing up and down the shore. "Maybe he didn't come here after all."

A small log cabin was visible through the trees. As Kay turned her head to look at it, she saw a young man and a girl emerge from the doorway. They did not see the rowboat but stood arm in arm looking out across the water.

"Ben, is that the couple you mentioned?" she asked.

"Yes, they didn't want anyone to know they were here, so they paid Smoky to keep quiet about it. They didn't give me anything, so I'm not bound by any promise."

"Ben! Let me off here!" Kay said suddenly.

Wendy and Betty looked at their friend in astonishment but asked no questions. Ben brought the boat close to a big rock and Kay stepped out onto shore.

"I'll be back in a minute," she promised.

Kay moved quietly up the path until she stood near the doorway of the cabin. She had acted on a hunch, and as she stared at the couple she realized she was right.

"I've found Norman Sewell and Shirley Hoffman!" she thought, her heart beating fast with excitement. "They look just like the photographs Mrs. Vernon showed me."

Kay stayed in her hiding place long enough to hear the girl call her companion Norman. The last doubt about their identity was erased when in their conversation, the pair mentioned that they had eloped.

Kay quietly returned to the boat. Although she was very excited, she knew better than to tell Ben Wheeler.

"Did you see Smoky anywhere?" he asked as she stepped into the boat.

Kay shook her head. "No, but I'd like to wait here a few minutes. He might come later."

Ben kept the boat in the shadow of the trees. Kay suggested that he look around the island himself. When Ben had left she quickly told the twins what she'd found.

"Don't tell Ben," she cautioned as they saw him returning. "And if we have a chance later to talk with Norman and Shirley, don't let them know that we know who they are."

For another ten minutes the four waited in the boat. Then Kay pointed to a canoe coming toward the beach.

"Is that Smoky?" she asked Ben.

"It looks like his canoe, all right!"

Watching from their hiding place, they saw Hagerty beach his craft.

"He has the box!" Wendy whispered excitedly. "It's in the bottom of the canoe! Let's jump him!"

"No! Let's wait!" Kay cautioned.

Smoky pulled the canoe far out of the water. Leaving the box, he walked quickly up the path toward the cabin.

"Now is our chance!" Kay decided. "Row around to the beach, Ben, and don't splash your oars!"

After Ben had brought the boat into shallow water, Kay jumped out. She dragged the canoe across the sand into the water and when it floated she tied it to her own boat with a rope.

"Do the couple have a boat, Ben?" she asked.

"Yes, they keep one hidden over there in the bushes to your right."

"See if you can find it," Kay said, looking anxiously in the direction of the cabin. "Row it over here and tie it to the canoe. Be quiet."

"I get the idea," Ben said with a grin. "Smoky can't swim a stroke, and without a boat he'll be stuck here on the island!"

"And so will the Sewells," Kay added under her breath.

"Kay, you think like a computer," Betty declared

admiringly. "Everything is working out. We have the box, Smoky is as good as caught, and the Sewells have been found!"

"It may not turn out as well as we want," Kay said soberly. "Why doesn't Ben hurry?"

He appeared at last, rowing the Sewell boat around a bend of the island. He tied it to the canoe, and with the two boats in tow, they started across the river toward the opposite shore.

"So far, so good," Kay grinned. "I don't think anyone saw us leave the island."

Wendy looked anxiously at the canoe which was tossing in the rough water.

"Aren't you afraid it may be swamped?" she asked Kay. "It would be terrible if we lost the box."

"I wish I had taken it out before we started across the river," Kay answered. "I'll get it now."

"No, it's too dangerous," Betty protested.

"Hold my hand and I'll be able to make it easily," Kay said confidently. "I'm not going to risk losing that box."

With Betty and Wendy giving support, she stepped up on the boat seat. From there Kay was able to step into the canoe.

She reached down to pick up the metal box. At that very moment the canoe was hit by a swell caused by a motorboat some distance away. The canoe bobbed wildly.

"O-oh!" cried Kay, hugging the box. "It's going over!"

XXV

The Crowley Fortune

As Kay tried to balance herself in the canoe, Betty and Wendy reached out and steadied it as best they could. Then the wave swept on toward shore and the water was smooth again. Kay climbed back into the boat with the precious box, breathing a sigh of relief as she sat down again.

A surprise awaited the girls when they reached the mainland. Shortly after Kay left the cottage, Bill had arrived. He and Mrs. Tracey immediately went to the river, and waited on the shore for them.

Kay took her mother and Bill aside, and told them her unexpected discovery. As a result of their little conference, a long distance telephone call was made to the Sewell family. Bill then went for the local police and went with them across the river in a police launch.

Smoky Rover tried to elude the police, but was finally cornered near the Sewell cabin. He put up a fierce struggle, but was subdued and handcuffs were slipped over his wrists.

The Sewells watched the struggle from the safety of their cabin. They were shocked to learn that Hagerty was a thief, and even more upset when one of the policemen, after examining the furniture in their cabin, told them that nearly every piece had been stolen.

"We bought these things from Mr. Hagerty,"

Norman Sewell declared. "We thought he had the right to sell them."

"I hope we won't be arrested," Mrs. Sewell murmured anxiously. "We can explain everything."

They were given a chance to do that the following day when both fathers arrived by plane. The couple welcomed their parents with open arms, and Mr. Sewell and Mr. Hoffman couldn't stay angry when they saw how happy Norman and Shirley were together.

Everyone praised Kay for the clever way she had trapped Smoky Rover. Mrs. Vernon congratulated her, saying that Kay should take up detective work as a career.

With the Crowley box finally in her possession, Kay intended to telephone the sisters. As it turned out, she didn't have a chance to. The two women arrived unexpectedly in the village. They had gotten so homesick that they were determined to spend their last days in their own house.

The sisters hardly dared to hope that Kay had found their precious box. They were overjoyed when she brought it to their cottage. Her mother, Bill and the twins came along.

"Wait, please," Henrietta Crowley requested as the visitors started to leave. "We want you all to see the contents of the chest."

"We don't know what's inside of it ourselves," Maud admitted as she fumbled nervously with the fastenings.

"You've never opened it?" Kay asked in amazement.

"Never. This box was left in our keeping by our brother Jack," Maud explained. "He ran away when he was young, and visited his home only three times after that. He was a little wild, and the family never talked about him."

"The last time he came home was over ten years ago," Henrietta took up the story. "He said he was going to South America and live in the jungles there. But we never knew when to believe him, and we hadn't heard from him since we received a card three Christmases ago."

"Until," Maud went on, "Jack Breen came to see us at the Thornton Home. He tried to find us here at the beach, but we had already left. He was bringing us news of our brother."

"On his trip to South America," Henrietta explained, "he met a doctor who worked far back in the jungle with the natives. This man had treated our brother before his death two years ago. He gave Mr. Breen a letter to us from Jack and a sort of will."

"The will said that the box contained everything needed to prove we were his beneficiaries, and insurance policies made out to us," Maud added.

"When we couldn't get back to dig the box up ourselves," Henrietta continued, "we asked you to do it for us. We'll never be able to thank you for finding the box, and then saving it from Hagerty. The box may mean that we won't have to go back to the Thornton Home."

Maud had succeeded in unfastening the lid, and as she raised it, a dead silence fell on the group. With trembling fingers the old lady lifted out a solid gold statue, a sparkling necklace, and several large, lustrous pearls.

"Are they genuine?" she gasped.

"Offhand, I would say they are worth a small fortune," Bill answered, fingering one of the stones.

"And here are the insurance papers," Henrietta murmured, taking a packet from the box. "Please look at them, Mr. Tracey," she requested.

"Your brother left a one-hundred-thousand-dollar

insurance policy," Bill said after he had studied the papers for a moment.

"Are we to inherit that?" Henrietta asked, dazed by the sudden good fortune.

"Yes, the policy is made out to you and your sister jointly," Bill told her.

Maud sagged into the nearest chair and began to cry. But her tears were tears of joy rather than of grief.

"Henrietta and I will be able to spend our last days here," she murmured. "We'll buy back our furniture from Mr. Wake and we'll be able to live respectably once more. Oh, it was so good of Jack to have remembered us at the end. He was a fine man at heart and I think we misjudged him."

Kay found it difficult to keep from smiling at this abrupt change of attitude toward the wandering brother. She went over to look into the box, and noticed that the sisters had failed to see another sheaf of papers in the very bottom.

"This looks like an old manuscript," she said. Maud Crowley lifted it out.

"Jack never wrote anything that long," Henrietta declared with conviction. "He seldom sent us letters because he felt it was too much trouble to write."

As Kay turned the first page of the manuscript, a slip of paper fell to the floor. She picked it up and read aloud:

"'Benson lost the bet. He said too that no one could crib his manuscript. But I did. He stole most of his information from Ezra Swope anyway so he should be the loser. Ha-ha-ha! Jack Crowley.'"

"Why, that doesn't make sense at all," Henrietta murmured.

"I think it does," Kay said. "The title of this manuscript is 'The History of Hadley County.' Chief

Benson and Ezra Swope both wrote such a history, and I understand they had a private bet that each would be the first to have his manuscript published. Ezra won when his rival's history disappeared."

"I still don't understand," Henrietta said, looking deeply perplexed.

"I think your brother played a joke on Chief Benson," Kay explained tactfully. "He must have taken the manuscript and hidden it in this box. Benson naturally accused Swope."

"But why should our brother do such a thing?" Maud murmured.

"Probably he had his own private bet about the affair. I understand that many people were interested in the rivalry between Swope and Benson. At any rate, this message completely clears Ezra Swope."

"You mustn't tell anyone," Maud said quickly.

"But you can't let an innocent man suffer!" Kay exclaimed.

She then told her how Chief Benson, believing that Ezra Swope had taken the manuscript, tried to avenge himself upon the son. Henrietta and Maud felt very sorry for Henry Swope, but couldn't bring themselves to allow Kay to expose what their brother had done.

It took two days for the Crowley sisters to finally conquer their pride and go with Kay to the police station. There they told everything they knew to Chief Benson, who seemed disappointed when he learned the truth. However, he was glad to have his manuscript again and admitted to Kay that he had been wrong about Henry Swope.

Both Smoky Rover and Ben Wheeler were brought to trial for their theft, but thanks to Bill Tracey's skillful defense, Ben went free while Smoky Rover got a long prison sentence. It was arranged for Ben to study in a trade school before he went back west. And in many ways he showed Kay and Bill his gratitude for everything they'd done for him.

From the Sewell family Kay received a substantial reward. A few weeks later Bill received a smaller reward when he succeeded in finding the paintings stolen from Burnham Quay.

After so much excitement, Kay and the twins were glad to have some peace and quiet. They went for long hikes and picnics and spent hours reading. One afternoon as they relaxed on the beach, Kay said, "I'm so happy about the way everything turned out. The Crowley sisters have their fortune, Ezra Swope is cleared, and Ben Wheeler has a new start and he'll go back to the west that he loves."

"Yes," Wendy nodded, "he belongs there." She began to quote softly:

> *"It's the white road westward is the road I must tread*
> *To the green grass, the cool grass, and rest for heart*
>   *and head,*
> *To the violets and the brown brooks and the*
>   *thrushes' song,*
> *In the fine land, the west land, the land where I*
>   *belong."'*

"Just think," Kay remarked when Wendy finished the poem, "if we had followed that message in the sand dunes saying 'Danger, don't dig here,' so many of these things never would have happened."